Amazing Grace

Heaven's Gift

Marsha Barth

Robert D. Reed Publishers

Robert D. Reed Publishers • Bandon, OR

Robert D. Reed Publishers
P.O. Box 1992
Bandon, OR 97411
Phone: 541-347-9882; Fax: -9883
E-mail: 4bobreed@msn.com
Website: www.rdrpublishers.com

Editor: Cleone Reed
Editorial Consultant: Michael Barth
Illustrations and story: Marsha Barth
Designer: Amy Cole
Cover: Cleone Reed

Soft Cover ISBN: 978-1-63821-500-4
EBook ISBN: 978-1-63821-501-1

Library of Congress Control Number: 2021941842

Designed and Formatted in the United States of America

Dedication

To my precious husband, Mike,
whose love has always held me,
words have always encouraged me,
and support has always believed in me ...

Table of Contents

Acknowledgments

O h, the splendor of Heaven! How can we ever truly understand all that awaits us on this beautiful journey. Truly, I thank our great God, our Savior, who has prepared a way for us to an eternal home. I thank Him that as a small child, His reality became an inspiration to my soul and led me through the many hardships of life, teaching me that His love is unconditional, His grace never ending, His mercy always hovering near, and His power was mine to overcome. I thank Him for the simple vision of this wonderful place that He has prepared for all who love and will serve Him here below—this place called Heaven. And I thank Him for His precious word that describes it all so beautifully. What a wonderful promise of eternity and joy.

To my dear husband, Mike, to whom this book is dedicated, I sincerely thank and acknowledge you for all of your hard work supporting me. Often, you are the one who has pushed me out of the comfort of the nest so that I could learn to fly.

I would be amiss without mentioning my beautiful family. In all of the trials of my life, it is my family who has always encouraged me to do more than I had ever thought I could do. From my Grammas, Momma, and Bucky; my dear brothers—Don, Terry, and Pat; my dear Aunt Joan who always has prayed for me, and so many others who have always believed in me, I sincerely thank you.

To my wonderful children, Mike and Missy, Jen and Jason—I thank you for your love and support. To my beautiful grandchildren—Ethan, so strong, and caring; Jayden, our happy one; Jadon, whom God has heard; our Colin, victorious and beloved; Benjamin, the son of our right hand; Isaac, our courageous one who makes us all laugh; Matthew, our gifted and brave one; to our Savannah, our beautiful rose (who loves pink) and our only girl; to Zachary, who is our rock; and to baby Evan, our mighty warrior—you are all my sunshine and joy.

I am so thankful for all of my friends, who have always been there for me. Some have crossed over to that beautiful shore and await me there, while others have believed in me and encouraged me many times in this wonderful work that God has called me to do. To all of you, your love has carried me.

And last but truly not the least are my wonderful publishers. Thank you Bob and Cleone for all that you have done for me. You have become my dear friends. Thank you for always working with me, through the edits, the cover, and the hard work that goes into publishing of which so many are unaware. Thank you always for your kindness and support.

A warm thank you to all of my readers who continue to support me—may you truly be blessed as you read *Amazing Grace: Heaven's Light*.

Preface

Mention heaven and you will get many different reactions. Some will be curious, others puzzled, some excited, and still others hesitant. To many, heaven is a place of which fairy tales are made—a place that is surreal or even more so, a place of fantasy. Heaven, to many, seems too far away and so unrelated to their current life that it hardly enters into their conscious thoughts.

It is interesting also to see the reaction of those whom I love when I mention writing a book about heaven. Some immediately think of death while others ask, "How can you write about heaven? You have never been there." And they are right. You can't get to heaven without dying, and how do you write about a place you haven't seen? How do you write about a place having such limited detailed information and where no one has visited and come back to discuss their trip?

But wonder if we could just for a moment, pause from this life, slow our hurried pace, take a deep breath, and enter heaven's gates? Wonder if we could get just a glimpse of all that awaits us? Wonder if we could lay down this heavy mantle of life for just a moment and get a vision of what "true life" really is? Wonder how our perception of this life would change if we would realize this temporal life is only for the preparation of an eternal life? Wonder what insight we would gain if we realized someday this earthly life was the fantasy world and heaven is for real? Can we begin to envision all that truly awaits us on that blessed other side?

To respond to some of those reactions, my first remark is usually with a chuckle, "I am not rushing my reservation." And to quote, Sam Levenson, "If you die in an elevator, be sure to push the up button." But, I always come back to the question, "Wonder if?"

Amazing Grace: Heaven's Light is a short novel portraying the reality of a real heaven. Many of the characters in the book are those who are in my other two books, *The Shattering* and *The Shattering II*. Here, within these pages, we find the closure of all closures. Here we find the many answers to "wonder if?" Wonder if, heaven is for real? Wonder if, we truly live again? Wonder if, heaven so surpasses what we had ever thought or dreamed about? Wonder if, heaven is not a dull and boring place where we live a hum-drum existence, as some may think, but it is the most exciting and invigorating life we could ever imagine? Wonder if, heaven is more than we ever hoped for: a place of complete rest, complete peace, and complete love; a place where every sense that we experience today is taken to a new level; where we don't see the beauty, but we feel the beauty; where we don't hear the music, but we live the music; where we don't just enter the portals of heaven, but where heaven becomes our home.

All of this is too vast for our human and finite mind to envision and behold. But here, there is the heavenly light. Here we meet the epitome of everything our very souls have longed for all of our lives and could not find. Here we meet our Savior and God. Here we understand all the mysteries of life. Here all of our questions are answered. Here we meet, once again, those who have gone before us.

Amazing Grace: Heaven's Light is a book of fiction, but it is not a book of fantasy. It is not written to be a theological book or to answer all of your questions. I have deliberately not capitalized the pronouns referring to God or the words heaven or hell. I wanted you to experience *him* as the one true Father in a personal relationship. Yes, *He* is the Alpha and Omega, the Beginning and the End. He is the Everlasting Father, the Prince of Peace, the Mighty God, Counselor, and our precious Jesus. He is all of this and more. But you may not understand *Him* as these, but you can understand *him* as a true father who wants to take you to the secret place, to dwell under the shadow of *his* love.

Amazing Grace: Heaven's Light is written so your eyes may get a glimpse of the reality of heaven, the reality of a God who loves you more than you could have ever imagined, that you may know you matter to Him more than life itself. From the beginning of creation, you were His sole purpose, His sole goal, His sole reason for creating the universe. Yes, you do matter!

Come with me and take a journey into *Amazing Grace* ...

Choices?

chapter

1

> *"Consider how precious a soul must be*
> *when both God and the devil are after it."*
> ~ Charles Spurgeon.

Startled, Julie awoke and sat up straight in her bed. As her heart raced within her she could feel its incessant beating within her chest. She glanced around the darkness of her bedroom and then laid back down.

Julie lay awake in the stillness of the night. Sleep felt far from her as she snuggled down into the warmth of her blankets. Even though her heart had now calmed within her, she remained wide awake.

Her thoughts raced back and forth as she lay quietly. They bounced around in her head, ricocheting through her mind, jumping from the loving thoughts of her family and grandchildren to the many things she should get done the next day. Julie was older now, much older many would say. Julie, however, refused to accept old. Once, her daughter had told her, "Mom you're getting old."

But Julie had given her a big smile and simply rebutted, "Er."

"What?" her daughter replied laughing.

"Er," Julie repeated, grinning, "Old-er. I won't claim old."

And yet, here she was in this stage of her life, "older," much older. Julie reflected on the many seasons of her life as she lay in the quietness of the night. She would often lay in her bed at night and remember the awesome journey God had led her on throughout her lifetime. So many seasons of life, full of beauty, hardships, battles, and victories. Regardless of how much "older" she would live to be, it had been a great journey, one she would not have changed. Through the many seasons of sorrow, all had served a purpose.

Julie felt a loving peace come over her. It covered her completely, wrapping her in its warmth. She snuggled once again down into her blankets. Her thoughts drifted now to the dream that had awakened her.

It was a strange dream—not a bad dream, or even scary, just different than any she had ever had. Julie was a dreamer. All of her life she had dreams. Many were dreams of value, of meaning. Some were often warnings, or inspirational, encouraging, or a note of correction. God would often speak to her through her dreams. But this dream was totally different than any she could remember.

The dream started in the midst of a beautiful garden.

Julie was walking through its meandering paths. The sun was brightly shining. Even in the dream, she could feel the sun's warm rays beat down upon her. As she walked, she could not help but notice the beautiful flowers. They were unlike any she had ever seen. She stopped and touched the soft petals, almost as if to see if they were real, or maybe not. They seemed to be iridescent. She could not begin to describe their colors as the colors would change intermittently.

As Julie walked, she could feel this was a place unlike any she had ever visited. In her dream, she was no longer "older," nor was she old. She was young again, carefree, without a care in the world.

The dream was so real, Julie thought, as she turned in her bed and snuggled down once again under the warm covers. As sleepy as she was, Julie still wanted to remember the dream so she could journal it the next day. She didn't want to forget any of it. Her tired mind once again returned to the dream.

> *As Julie wandered down the path, she continued to be mesmerized by the beauty surrounding her. It was a strange yet beautiful place. "Where am I?" Julie whispered to herself.*
>
> *The path led her out of the garden and to a crossroad of many paths to choose from. Julie stood looking at the many paths before her. So many paths to choose from, all going in different directions. All seemed to bid her to come. But somehow in the dream, as it had been so in her life, she seemed to know which one she had to choose. It appeared to her as a path that was less worn; a path seeming to lack the luster or even the beauty of the other paths. But somehow Julie knew this was the path she should take.*
>
> *As Julie turned and started to walk down the path, she noticed it was rocky with steep inclines, and even more treacherous declines. She maneuvered the ever-turning curves that led her down a steep hill. Julie knew she had never been to this place before, and yet it all seemed so vaguely familiar to her.*

Julie could feel herself now beginning to drift into a deep sleep, but she deliberately stirred herself and once again turned in her bed. "I've got to remember the part that woke me up," she mumbled, instructing herself to stay awake.

Julie continued to walk down the rugged path. She wondered, why had she chosen this path? Had she really chosen this path? All she knew was that there was a leading, a bidding as such, which had drawn her to walk in this direction and that she must walk it.

She was relieved to come to a point in the path where it leveled off. She walked slowly, catching her breath. It now narrowed and became much smoother. Julie once again began to see more beautiful flowers along the way. They swayed in a gentle breeze and seemed to beckon her forward.

Julie now noticed there were other paths connected to the one she was on. She felt it tempting to maybe choose one of these. Her path, though beautiful, was still very rocky in places. Julie could see in the distance that there were many steep mountains ahead of her if she was to remain on it. The other ones seemed much more inviting. They beckoned her to come with almost an enticing excitement of adventure and intrigue.

Julie stopped and paused at one point and considered that maybe she was meant to pick the path veering to the right. She couldn't help notice the beauty it presented to her. The ground was covered with a soft velvety moss. Julie took off her shoes and proceeded down this new path. She could feel the moss softly between her toes, cool and soft, beckoning her to choose this way. Julie took another step, feeling sure this was the path she was to take, and then another. She smiled as she took yet another step and continued to go forward. But suddenly, Julie began to feel uneasy as the path grew dim and darkened. The flowers which had first appeared were no longer there. The path became very rugged and Julie could no longer see where she was going. The sun had disappeared and there was no warmth. She began to feel a chill come over her. The peaceful presence surrounding her before was gone. Julie paused and looked around her, but everything was dark and there was no light in the distance.

Julie abruptly stopped walking as the very presence of darkness seemed to encompass her. She felt lost, truly lost. Julie turned and began to run. However, her legs felt heavy, as if attached to lead weights. She struggled to lift them as she ran. She glanced behind her as if to see if someone was chasing her. All of a sudden she felt such a presence of evil, an indescribable evil. She attempted to run faster and faster. She was out of breath and her legs still wouldn't move the way she commanded them. She was running in the dark, not able to see where she was going. "What happened to the light?" she exclaimed loudly, glancing once again behind her as she continued to try to run.

And then she saw it. Not so far in the distance glimmered a faint light, so faint she could barely see it. Julie squinted her eyes tightly as if to be sure it was real. As she continued to move her heavy legs forward, the light became brighter, much brighter. She no longer felt the presence of evil following her.

It was here that she had awoken with a start. *I have to journal this dream tomorrow,* Julie thought. *It surely must have a meaning to it.* Julie snuggled down under her covers once again, still wondering what the meaning of the dream was. But, as she had so often done throughout her lifetime, Julie began to whisper a gentle prayer, "I do know, dear Jesus, you were the light that I was running to." Julie then fell into a deep and peaceful rest.

11

Coming Home...

chapter

2

Julie blinked her eyes and squinted. The light was so bright. She couldn't help wonder if she was dreaming. It was as if she had fallen asleep, awoken, and was totally unaware of where she was. But once again, she felt an aura surround her whole being.

Everything was so pure and very intense. Julie felt as if she could burst from the inside out. She then began to feel a deep rest come upon her. It was a rest that seemed to settle down upon her and cover her in a blanket of comfort—a complete rest encompassing her whole being. Julie closed her eyes, letting herself fade into this oblivion of peace. When she opened them, she understood that all things were somehow different, as if all things had become new.

Julie found herself walking. Her heart overflowed. Never had she experienced such an overwhelming presence of love. It radiated all around her. The intensity of it engulfed her until she literally glowed in its presence. This was love in its purest form. It was filled with peace and joy filling Julie with rapture.

Where am I? Julie thought. She wondered if she was asleep or awake. *Was this more of the dream? Was she still dreaming?* Julie rubbed

13

her eyes and squinted them once again. The light was bright and full of warmth.

Julie continued to walk slowly. *Surely, I must be dreaming*, she thought. "Where am I?" she spoke in a quiet whisper.

This was a place like no other. As Julie walked, she passed others along the way. Some she knew; some she did not. Even with those whom she didn't know, there was an aura surrounding them over-flowing with that same presence of love. It was a love surrounding her, radiating throughout her very being, filling her soul with a completeness she had always seemed to long for.

Julie hurried at first, anxious to see more, know more, and experience more. She pressed on gently as she passed through the crowd surrounding her. She knew so many of them. There were no distinct memories at first, just an assuredness and a certainty that somewhere they had impacted her life with good. Somehow, Julie instinctively knew this, as she also seemed to know, that here, there was no sorrow. The throng of people still encircled her. Their presence alone seemed to cause her to glide effortlessly through the crowd.

As she gazed at the bright light in the far distance, which drew her evermore nearer, she could feel, more than see, the fulfillment of what she knew was her heart's desire. From the time she was a small child in the little country church sitting upon the top of the mountain where she lived, it was there she had first met him. Julie could remember the very day she had asked him to come into her heart; once, when she was only five years old, and again when she was eight. She had felt this same presence of God, even then, bidding her to come to him, as she shyly had stepped out into the aisle and walked down to the altar. It was that day, so long ago, that in her childlike innocence and faith, she had asked him to come into her heart. Throughout all the many years of her struggles, failures and sorrows, he had become her hope and heart's desire. Somehow she knew now, as she had known then, that he awaited her.

It was as if she was walking on air. Julie felt as if she was flying. There was an orchestra of music and singing filling the air. It was the purest music Julie had ever heard. It was all so different than any music she had ever known. It was as if the music was three-dimensional. *Here,* she thought, *you didn't really hear the music; you felt the music. It carried you.*

Julie's instinct was to run, but as her legs moved, she realized it was not their movement propelling her forward. As she gained momentum, the air brushed passed her, gently blowing her hair with a warm breeze. She could feel the warmth as if there were rays of sunlight beating down upon her, warming her very being.

There was a beautiful fragrance filling the air. A sweet indescribable aroma, it tantalized all of her senses. She closed her eyes and took in a deep breath, engulfing the full intensity of the fragrance.

Julie continued to let herself fade into this oblivion of peace and love as it enveloped her. She opened her eyes widely and glanced down at her feet as they continued to glide forward. Everything was so real, so true, and yet everything appeared transparent. Through her feet, she could see the streets of gold. She turned her head to the side, looking back and forth. As she continued, she noticed there was still a throng of people encircling her. To Julie's surprise, she could see completely through the people. There were giant walls made of pure jasper. Julie had never seen anything so beautiful. There were no words to describe the splendor or beauty appearing before her. No words could describe the presence radiating around her and seeming to carry her forward.

Julie closed her eyes once again as she approached the beautiful light. Everything in her midst began to intensify and surround her until she was totally engulfed by that same strong presence. As Julie opened her eyes, nothing could have prepared her for what she saw. Appearing before her stood a beautiful waterfall. As it flowed before her, its glistening waters reflected what appeared to be rays of light shining like sparkling diamonds before it hit the river below, where its white foam encircled the protruding rocks.

Where was she? She continued to wonder as she looked around. The sound of the waterfall, as loud as it was, did not drown out the other sounds of this heavenly place. The wind blew gently, moving what appeared to be trees in a swaying motion, which seemed to keep in time to a distant song that ever so softly filled the air. Julie pricked her ear upward towards the sweet music as if to listen more clearly. But try as she may, she could only hear it ever so softly. It was in itself as a gentle breeze sweeping over her very soul. And though she was alone, she felt as if she was in the midst of thousands. She looked around but no one was there. Julie slowly walked over to a large rock and sat down, feeling like she could stay there forever. The beauty, the fragrance filling the air, the presence of love, peace, and joy—it all seemed more than her senses could receive.

"It's like that at first," a soft voice gently spoke to her. Julie turned to see the figure before her. She was not startled by the sound of his voice. It was as if he was meant to be there. Julie thought for a moment. There was no fear, no dismay, no sorrow, and no apprehension. "They don't exist here," the voice said lovingly, as if reading Julie's mind.

Julie stood up and walked over to him and took his outstretched hand. She looked into his face. As their eyes met, she smiled. He smiled back. And when he did, it was as if billows of love were released from him floating over Julie and encompassing both of them in a fine mist of shimmering light. She knew him. No words needed to be spoken. Julie continued to gaze into his eyes. "It's you," she exclaimed, her heart filled with rapture. "It's really you," she repeated.

He then took her into his arms and softly said, "It is I".

Julie let herself collapse into his loving embrace and laid her head upon his chest. "The Alpha and Omega," Julie whispered. She had come home.

In the Garden

chapter

3

"For now we see through a glass, darkly;
but then face to face: now I know in part;
but then shall I know even as also I am known."
~ 1 Corinthians 13:12

ulie sat quietly in the garden as heaven's rays shone down upon her. The garden was her favorite place. Julie did not know how long she had been in heaven; it seemed awhile. But here, there was no true essence of time. It was more the familiarity that defined time, more than time itself.

Julie met so many people who she had once known. What was so amazing was, without even knowing them, she knew them. She knew them as they were known. Yet, though there were no memories as such, there was a knowledge of memories, but without sorrow. She could not recall if she had a mom, a dad, brothers or sisters. But, yet she would know, if she met one of them. She knew who they were. Nothing had to be explained. There was no need to. She just knew. And there was no sorrow, no tears of pain; just joy when meeting the souls who had impacted her life.

Julie recalled the first time she had met and truly known someone whom she had loved. She was walking along a river bank where flowers flowed over its sides in a waterfall of beauty. The colors were so intense, it was as if they beckoned her to come and sit in their midst. Julie walked slowly down its bank and let the fragrance filling the air flow over her soul. She sat down along the edge and leaned back on her arms, closed her eyes, and tilted her head back. Heaven's light radiated down upon her, engulfing her, and then flowing over her in soothing waves of warmth. She opened her eyes and watched aimlessly as the water rushed past her in gentle ripples, moving, but yet as if standing still. The river appeared as calm and still as glass—smooth, shining, glistening in the light.

There was a quiet rustle beside her and Julie turned to see what was there. Everything was as if normal, as if it just was. She wasn't startled to see the soul who was approaching her, only surprised that he was alone. Usually, Julie would feel the throng of many souls as she would walk through the many paths enjoying and discovering all of the beauties which surrounded her. However, she had never met a soul who was all alone. As he neared, it seemed quite normal as anything else Julie had experienced. Life here just seemed to always unfold before you, and as it did, it always seemed right and proper.

Julie started to get up, but the soul gestured kindly with his hand for her to remain seated. As he sat down beside her, Julie turned to face him. His hair was snow white and his eyes bluer than she could have ever remembered. She instantly felt the familiarity of his spirit as she began to feel a joy rise up within her. She turned to face him more directly and looked deeply into his eyes. He said not a word as he watched Julie study him. Julie took her hand and touched his worn face. It was rough and even a little bristly and felt unshaven, and yet soft, as she gently caressed his cheek. Julie smiled a broad smile and said, "I know you."

The old man smiled back, his intense blue eyes engulfing Julie in his fatherly love. Julie smiled as his love encompassed her. She knew before he even spoke, who he was. "I promised you I'd be the first to greet you when you got here," he reminded her kindly. Julie fell into his arms, which gently wrapped themselves around her, and both began to release the pure joy of seeing each other. And yet, there were no tears, just the infiltrating presence of love. "I did promise you that," he continued, as they paused and looked at one another.

"I made you promise me," Julie said, with a little laugh. "I couldn't let you go without knowing that I'd see you again, Bucky."

"I know," Bucky replied, as he touched her face. Julie sat and continued to share with her stepfather—the one who had given her the only true father's love that she had ever known.

Julie paused and closed her eyes. She heard a chorus of angels singing a song, and though she did not know it, she sang along with them. Her voice blended in with the heavenly chorus, and as it did, the presence of love was magnified in the praises that were being sung. When Julie opened her eyes, she wasn't surprised when she saw a woman sitting beside her instead of her Bucky. The woman looked deeply into Julie's eyes where both of their souls met. Julie wrapped her arms around the woman and laid her head on her chest. The woman gently caressed Julie. Though there were no tears, the emotions of the love that they had shared from the past, with the purity of love existing here, became one. The love flowed from her soul unto her mom, and her mom's love flowed from her soul to Julie.

"It's you, Momma," Julie exclaimed, as she looked into her mom's eyes. "I knew I'd find you here. I knew I would!" Julie could see her mom's expression as from the days of old, the expression of when her mom could not speak for being so filled with emotions. Julie knew this familiar look; it had always expressed how much a soul can love another—how proud a soul can feel for another—how sure a soul could believe in another. This was the bond of love, and the true power of such a love. Julie knew how much her mom's love had impacted and carried her through some of the darkest days of her life. Even though there were no specific memories of those sad days, there was an essence of knowing that there had been some great tumult and that they had come through it together.

That's the way it was here. You knew in part, yet you knew in whole. No longer did you look through a glass dimly, but you saw clearly with full understanding. It could never have been felt in the natural. This could only come to pass in the spirit. Ethel placed Julie's hand into hers as she had done so many times when Julie was a child. They sat and stared at the crystal clear water flowing past them for a long time before speaking. "Are there more?" Julie asked her mom, loving that special feeling of being a child again.

Ethel looked at her daughter once again and drew her near to her side. "Yes, Honey," she answered. "There are many more."

A Favorite Place

chapter
4

"Death ends a life, not a relationship."
~ Mitch Albom

Everything was so real. Julie thought it strange that in her mortal life, heaven had seemed so mystical, so far away, and so vague. *What could be more real than life itself?* But in heaven, Julie felt life in a way she had never experienced before. It was as if life, before now, was dull, surreal, and far away. As if life then was in a different spectrum—vague and unreal, like a dream. It was only when Julie met a familiar soul, one who had impacted her old life, that the past would become real once again.

Julie walked into what appeared to be a small kitchen full of people. She smiled, as she remembered the familiar scene. She watched an older woman begin to shew the others out of her kitchen. She beckoned Julie to take a seat at the kitchen table as she turned her back to cook. Julie sniffed in the air and smelled the aroma of fresh homemade bread, mingled with the smell of eggs frying. A joy begin to fill her. This was a special reunion that she knew her heavenly Father had arranged just for her. Julie couldn't understand how she was able to know this, but she did. Julie sat and watched the older woman frantically cook, flipping her eggs with the greatest of ease, opening the oven door to remove the freshly baked bread and turning to place it on the table before Julie. She gave Julie a warm smile as she wiped her hands on her apron and took Julie's plate. She generously piled on the fried potatoes and eggs, and then placed the plate in front of Julie.

Julie smiled and watched as the older woman pulled out a chair and sat down. Their eyes met and locked together as they sat there entwined in the love that surrounded them. "Hi Gramma," Julie beamed, breaking the silence, still locked into her grandmother's gaze.

"Welcome home," the older woman spoke softly as she placed her hand on top of Julie's, and gave her a smile flooding Julie's heart full of the love that they had once shared.

Julie's favorite times were those spent with the one whom she had always known loved her. It was he that made it heaven. It was his presence and light that flowed throughout the heavenly realm and everywhere she went. She never left him on her excursions, as he was with her in spirit everywhere she went. She could always feel his abiding presence. It was this presence that would cause her soul to rest in a heavenly bliss that was not explainable in natural words but radiated throughout all of heaven. From the very first moment, when they had met face-to-face at the waterfall, she knew instantly that she had always known him and he her.

"Before you were in the womb, I knew you," he told her that day. Julie smiled and looked deeply into his eyes. His eyes were different than the eyes of the souls who she had met. When their eyes would meet, their souls would become one and all of the knowledge that they had shared together would just be known between them. However, when Julie would look into her Savior's eyes, she would become one with him. Her heavenly Father's eyes had no distinction or color, just love. They were pure love. Julie tried to describe them in her mind, and even in her heavenly spirit, but there was no way to describe them. They seemed to be iridescent, constantly changing, sparkling, and glimmering with a presence of love that she could hardly behold even with her spiritual eyes. Julie relinquished the idea of attempting to come up with a color that could define love.

Through all of the years she had lived, Julie had always felt and known his presence, heard his voice, and bathed in his love. He had always continued to encourage her to go forward—one more step, one more stand, one more battle. But never in her old form could she have experienced or have seen him this way. Her body would have been too fragile to partake in the fullness of this true and pure love and in the fullness of his being and presence.

Julie was now able to sit with him as he imparted the deeper things and answered her unasked questions. Often, he would just sit and bless her with his love and wait until she would ask him her questions, even though she felt that he already knew what she was going to ask. Ever so tenderly, so patiently, as she laid her head upon his chest, he stroked her hair and nurtured her with the love that she somehow knew from her life before, but never to this extent. Here everything was pure and untouched; therefore it really couldn't be compared to her past life. There she had felt only the earnest of his love, unlike here where she felt it completely.

There is no way to describe love in its purest form. It cannot be expressed. It can only be experienced. It was enough to enjoy these moments alone. If this was all there was to heaven, it would have been more than enough.

It always amazed Julie how things were never explained here, and yet somehow you would know and understand. But you would know and understand without feeling the sorrow. Words could not explain this, and Julie now understood why the Bible was not always explicit on so many of the specific details of heaven.

Julie smiled to herself as heavenly breezes brushed past her. "We would have never understood it," she said softly to Jesus.

"It is a peace that passes understanding," he answered lovingly.

Julie continued to sit quietly, thinking and pondering on this wonderful place called heaven. *Would she ever see all of it? Was there no true beginning or end?* Her mind wandered once again to a soul who she often met on her walks, but she had no knowledge of how their lives had impacted each other.

"So, what are you thinking, my little Jul?" Father asked.

Julie was quiet and pondered his question.

"You were always my pondering one," Jesus continued, placing his hand tenderly upon Julie's head and pressing it to his bosom. "You were my deep child, always trying to figure it out, always trying to understand it all." His hand gently stroked her hair. Julie felt so safe, loved, and secure. She let go, falling into his deep love and presence. She stayed there for what seemed forever. But here there was no time, only the feeling of the essence of time. Julie once again looked up into his loving eyes.

"There is a soul who I meet often," she started.

"And?" Jesus questioned softly.

"I can't explain it," Julie answered. "This soul is different."

"How?" Jesus asked.

"I know him, but I can't connect with him. I've met a few souls here like that, but with him it's such a strong impact. I feel like I should know him, but the knowledge is not there."

"And so this puzzles you?" he asked.

"Some," Julie replied softly.

Jesus pulled her gently close to him. "You were always my little girl who was so puzzled by life. You always wanted to understand everything, to somehow make all that was wrong, right."

"I still do," Julie answered, giving him her impish smile that had always melted his heart.

"Well," he said. "Here you know souls as they were known in your life then, but without the sorrow and pain. So you recognize each other and the impact you had upon each other. But some souls who impacted your life impacted your life in their unredeemed state. Some souls were never redeemed, and you will not meet them here because they chose not to be redeemed. But other souls were redeemed whom you had impacted. These are the souls you know and they know you."

"But there is one in particular," Julie continued.

"I know," Jesus answered and paused. "I've been waiting for you to talk to me about him. He talks to me often about you."

"Is he confused or puzzled, too?" Julie asked.

"No, because he knows the impact that you had upon his life. He doesn't have knowledge of the pain, because there is no pain here, but he has knowledge of the joy of being redeemed. And he knows that you played a part in that. He has a great joy, and feels a gratitude and love, for you," Jesus explained.

"Will I have, at some time, knowledge of who he is?" Julie asked.

"Maybe," Jesus answered kindly. "We understand all things better as they unfold before us. By and by you will understand."

A Special Reunion

chapter

5

"There is no remedy for love but to love more."
~ Henry David Thoreau

ulie began to realize that it never rained in heaven. She didn't know why she had not noticed or comprehended this before. In the stillness of what she would call morning, there was always a fine mist that arose from the stream beds and waterfalls. The light of heaven always shone brightly. It was never dreary or cloudy. The warmth of his presence always perpetuated through the mist, throughout the paths in the garden, in the meadows, and on the breadth of the shores.

Julie knew the splendor of heaven would never grow old with her, even if there had been such a thing in heaven as growing old. Every moment was fresh, alive, and full of new experiences. At times, when she thought she knew most of the souls in heaven, she would only turn to discover so many more. She often wondered why she hadn't seen them earlier, but then Jesus would remind her that not everyone she knew had come home yet. For Julie, it seemed as if she had been there forever, and yet in some ways, it seemed as if she had just arrived. She couldn't discern the two, because there was no such thing as time, and it was too difficult to put it into perspective. She remembered, in knowledge, that in her old life, infinity and forever seemed too complex for her mind to grasp. And now, being here, the knowledge of yesterday and tomorrow were too difficult for her to understand. Everything seemed to transform into an unexplainable sense of just knowing.

Julie walked through the gardens, meeting with many of those whom she had known. She also met with new souls who had impacted others whom she either knew or had read about. The day she had met Peter astounded her. He wasn't like what she had imagined when she had read about him in the Bible. He was a thousand times more vivid in character—vibrantly strong and yet earnestly compassionate.

There were always more and more people who she would meet along the way. One of her favorite experiences was to be part of the throng that would gather when a soul came home whom they had all known. It was a jubilee. The angels would sing a new song every time. Julie didn't think there could be anything more beautiful than a song that she'd hear, only to hear another one that would be even more beautiful.

One day, as Julie walked quietly through a meadow and towards a small river bed, she couldn't help but feel a familiarity. Not familiar because she had visited it before but familiar from her old life. She then rounded a bend in the river. The water sparkled as it flowed over the rocks and entered into a calm pool of water.

Julie continued to walk along the path. It was lined with flowers, beautiful flowers that she had never seen before. They were so full of indescribable colors. In her past, colors were mostly distinct, specifically red, blue, purple, pink, orange, and so on. But here, the colors were all of these in one, ever changing before her eyes.

Their fragrance was like none she had ever known. Again, in her past, smells were specific. A rose smelled like a rose. A lilac smelled like a lilac. But here all the scents were one, yet different, individual, but yet blended. Julie literally skipped down the path closer to the river's side. She never tired of this beautiful place. She reached down and picked up a flat stone and fingered it in her hand, letting its smooth surface roll through each finger individually. She glanced down at it and thought to herself, *perfect*. She raised her arm to throw the rock but stopped abruptly.

"This one would work better," a voice sounded behind her.

"No, I think this one would be the best," another chimed in.

"No one can beat this one," a third voice interrupted the others.

Julie turned around at the first sound of her visitors. Julie loved these moments in heaven, these personal encounters, these blessed reunions that she knew were arranged by her heavenly Father. Next to her personal special moments with the Father, she treasured these.

Julie stood and gazed at the three young men who stood before her. She knew them instantly. The love was so strong that she just stood and stared at them, and they at her. The light of heaven shone brighter upon them, as their love rose like a fine mist, covering them in its presence. Julie watched the men transform before her. It was almost like watching an old movie reel. First, they were children: Matt with his blond hair and blue eyes; Jerry with the rooster tail, the cowlick in his hair that had always stood straight up, and the customary black eye he so often sported; and Ronnie with his jet dark hair and dark brown eyes. Julie's eyes and heart filled with love and joy. She wondered if she had appeared as that little ragged girl with curly hair to them. Julie felt she would burst with feelings of love. She watched as they continued to transition before her eyes, from children to young men, to adults, and then as older men.

The light shone less brightly now as they took on their spiritual form while the presence of heaven's love continued to overshadow them.

"Wait up you guys!" Julie smiled as she let the familiar words, that she had so often said to them, spill from her mouth, and she ran to greet them.

"Wait up Julie," the three of them echoed back in unison, smiling.

Julie looked a little puzzled at first and then asked, "I made it here before you?"

"You always told us you wouldn't rush your reservation," Jerry laughed as he tightly embraced his sister. Julie hugged him with her whole heart, never wanting to let him go.

She paused and looked at Ronnie. Ronnie gave her a broad smile. Julie looked at her Ronnie. No longer did he bear the scars of pain and of the war that had worn and tortured him so in their past. No longer did his face languish, or was it etched with what Julie knew then, was great sorrow.

"My brother shall rise again," Julie quoted their private promise, which they had always shared together since he had come home from the war.

Julie ran to Ronnie and embraced him in her arms.

"Your brother rose again," Ronnie repeated the promise.

Julie then turned to Matt. She walked over to him and tousled his blond hair while peering into his deep blue eyes. Those eyes had shown Julie more love than any words they had ever spoken.

"We're home, Julie," Matt exclaimed as they embraced.

Julie, still holding the rock in her hand, excitedly proclaimed, "No!" to her brothers laughing. "This is the best rock of all for skipping," as she released the stone and watched it skim across the water's surface.

"We'll see about that," Jerry resounded as he skipped his rock across the still water.

"Watch this one," Ronnie called out as he released his rock.

"Ten skips," echoed Matt, as his rock soared across the water. The air filled with their joy and laughter as they shared the beautiful love that they had always known.

"Michaela"

chapter

6

*"There is no footprint too small
to leave an imprint on this world."*
~ Unknown

The choruses of angels and souls singing continually reverber-
ated throughout all of heaven. It was as if a pleasant savor
filled the air, mingling with all the sweet aromas of heaven. Here,
all the senses were one, and yet separate at the same time. What you
heard could also be felt, smelled, seen, and experienced. It was the
same with what you would see. It was as if you were truly seeing
everything in color for the first time.

When Julie had lived in her past life, she thought she had seen
things clearly and that they were so beautiful. But in heaven, everything was so different. Everything was pure, distinct, vivid, and
intense. It made the things of her past appear as black and white.
The intensity of the colors were not only seen, but you felt them.
Here you didn't just hear the music, you lived it. Here you didn't
just feel things, you absorbed them. Everything you felt, heard,
seen, or even tasted was in its purest form and it consumed your
whole being. Here, all was true, all was good.

Julie had loved the ocean in her past. She would hear the waves
beckon her as she walked along the shore. She would smell the
fresh air and feel the sand ooze between her toes. So it was, as she
walked along this heavenly shore. Often, she would be by herself.

Sometimes, she would meet the Father here, and at other times she would meet her family or friends. For Julie, it was a special place.

The portrait of this vast body of water that lay before her was nothing like the oceans of her previous life. Julie felt the warmth of heaven's light upon her. More than warming her body, she felt it to the depth of her very soul and spirit. It was heavenly light. Julie glanced out at the rumbling water, instinctively shading her eyes as if from the sun, and watched the waves roll in one by one. She glanced towards the horizon where the deep blue waters met the light blue sky. Her heavenly senses swept her away in the beauty of it all. The great white caps of foam broke into waves before her. The water gently came to rest at her feet, tickling and dancing around them, before rushing back into the deep. Julie let out a slight giggle and then turned to walk down the shore. But to her surprise, there it was, the most beautiful sight. In the distance a beautiful rainbow arched across the breadth of the sky on the far horizon. The beauty radiated through her.

Julie wondered how there could be so many souls encompassing heaven, and yet it was never crowded. She wondered how God could be so specific with fulfilling her every desire. She wondered how this awesome Father could spend so much time with her and still be with all of the others in the same way. Julie could never describe the essence of time in heaven's limitless infinity. And yet, God was always there, in a twinkling of an eye, omnipresent, omnipotent, all powerful, and all loving. She had shared this very thought with so many of her loved ones and friends here. They, too, had marveled at this.

It was the wonderful experience of knowing the full reality of God's love, and having the full knowledge that you not only mattered to God, but that you truly were his child, that made heaven so special. Julie paused to wonder as she so often did. When she would often meet with him in the garden, she would ask him about all of these things she pondered in her heart. Julie wondered if people truly knew that this is what awaited them here in heaven, that the things of their world would grow strangely dim and seem very insignificant and unimportant. She wondered how her former world could have been so different had the focus of life remained on the spiritual and not the physical. She marveled at the fallen world she had lived in, knowing and yet not knowing, satisfied and yet wanting. All of this, she would often discuss with the Father. Julie only wished that those she had left behind could truly know how very much they did matter. How it is redemption that sets the soul free and gives the soul identity—not the material things and physical gratifications.

Julie glanced into the distance. There appeared to be two people slowly approaching. They were so far away that they appeared as silhouettes against the bright blue sky. Julie felt her heart leap within her as the Father's presence and love increased around her. She knew, deep inside, this was going to be a special encounter.

At times, Julie would meet different souls amidst the throngs when they would all gather together. Though some she knew, she would often have no particular knowledge of the impact that they had had on her life. Some had impacted her life in small but important ways. Some had impacted her life in greater ways. Some had made her become a better person, or indirectly but powerfully, had changed her life's course. She remembered once meeting her old principal, Mr. Jenkins, who had taken her under his wing, believed in her, and had gotten her into college with a full scholarship. She remembered another time meeting her old Sunday school teacher, Mrs. Burkhart, who had taught her truths that had come back to rescue her years later. She also remembered meeting Ms. Dawson; sweet gray-haired Ms. Dawson from her childhood, who after church service would come to her with an angelic smile, and say, "How you doing, *Ole Faithful?*" At other times, it might have been a classmate she knew from first grade, or a lady who she had helped at one time with her groceries. Whatever the impact they had had on her previous life, or her on theirs, she knew. They knew. This created an ever-flowing and never-ending flow of an ineffable and inexpressible love the likes of which could never have been experienced in her other life.

But the reunions were usually separate from many of these meetings. The reunions were special times of reuniting, and the Father took great care to make these occasions special. At these wonderful times, it would be more than just meeting others. It was knowing that we had been loved and getting to acknowledge this. There was a purpose and knowledge revealed in these encounters also. Here, questions would be answered, which had not even been asked. Here, the victory that was won there was felt and experienced, not in part, but in true completion. The joy coming from these meetings connected the souls with each other and the Father in a realm that could never have been experienced by mankind.

Julie continued to peer down the shore as the two forms continued to walk slowly towards her. There was no hurry here. Julie could feel the love and knowledge of these souls increasing as they approached. She could now see that one was a small child, the other, a man who was very young. Julie loved meeting the children here. It was a strange thing that she had never seen infants or babies per se, as most of these were usually represented as small children if they had died as infants. Even though you would see a small child as young, you were always able to see their soul, which had no age. If a soul would reveal itself through a child, there was usually a specific reason for doing this: to either reveal the knowledge of who they were to you at that time in your life, or to reveal the familiarity and impact that they had had on your life then. The beauty of it all was that you were able to see their soul, who they truly were, regardless of age.

This was a different experience for Julie. She couldn't recall when she had ever felt such a strong knowledge of any soul who she had met in heaven, as the two who were continuing to come closer.

Julie had no idea of any element of time since she had come to heaven. She had no knowledge whether she had been in heaven for what would be considered a day, a week, a year, five years, or possibly twenty.

Julie smiled, as she stood waiting. She couldn't help but wonder if their anticipation was as great as hers. *Were they caught up in the same splendor that she was feeling?*

Then, all of a sudden, she saw them stop. Julie could now see in the distance; one of them was a little girl, the other a man, but she couldn't quite make out their features. The little girl who was holding the man's hand began to tug at his arm and pulled him near to her. The man bent down and the little girl spoke to him.

Julie watched, more than a little puzzled, as her heart began to fill with a joy she felt she couldn't contain. The closer they came, the greater the presence of love encompassed Julie. The man glanced at her from the distance. Julie couldn't make out the expression on his face. He then turned and nodded to the little girl. Julie wondered if he knew any more than she did. Somehow, Julie felt that the little girl was orchestrating this reunion through the Father.

Julie watched as the little girl began to move slowly away from the man. He stood and watched her, and then turned and sat down onto the sand. The little girl began to walk towards Julie, slowly at first, and then at a faster pace, and then into a full run.

Julie knelt down on one knee to catch the little girl who rushed into her arms. She held her tightly as the little girl wrapped her small arms around Julie's neck. Julie had no knowledge of who she was, and yet somehow she knew that she knew this child, probably even more than anyone else whom she had ever met in heaven. Julie could not let her go. Even the desire to look at this precious child couldn't tear her from Julie's arms. Julie stroked the little girl's long blonde curls. They were blonder than any of her other children's hair. Julie studied the small child as she continued to hold her. It was as if she had known her for only a short time, if at all, but also as if somehow she had known her all of her life. The confusion did not bother Julie. She knew the Father would reveal all things to her.

Slowly, the little girl released her grip from around Julie's neck and let her arms slowly slip to her side. Julie continued to hold the little girl in her arms and looked into her beautiful blue eyes. Julie could see into the child's soul, this beautiful, beautiful soul. Even though Julie's eyes were not yet enlightened, she recognized the deep love. Julie then let the little girl down.

"Come sit beside me," the little girl instructed in her childlike voice as she sat down and patted the sand beside her.

Julie sat down beside the little girl and took her hand into hers. Julie could not let go of the little girl. There was a special connection when they touched. The power of love was so strong. Julie sat, not seeing a need to talk.

After a while, the little girl spoke. "My name is Michaela."

"Well, hello, Michaela," Julie replied. She couldn't take her eyes off of this angelic child.

"I have someone who the Father wanted me to introduce you to," she continued in her childish voice. She pushed her bare feet into the sand.

"I see he's waiting down there," Julie continued.

"He's anxious to meet you," Michaela stated as she let go of Julie's hand and began to play in the sand.

Julie continued to watch the child playing and smiled. "Does he know me?" Julie asked.

"No," Michaela answered, smiling back at Julie. "But he will."

"I see," Julie answered, giving Michaela another big smile. The little girl warmed Julie's heart unlike any other.

"You know me, don't you?" Michaela asked.

"I do," Julie answered. "I know I do, but the Father has not made known the full knowledge of who you are completely."

Michaela turned from playing and patted her sandy hands together. She looked deep into Julie's eyes, deeper than anyone had ever looked into her eyes. Julie thought her heart would burst. Never had she felt such a knowledge without completion.

"The Father wanted it that way," Michaela answered Julie's unasked question.

"Oh, I see," Julie said, grinning from ear to ear.

"Come on," Michaela said eagerly as she jumped up and began to tug at Julie's arm to pull her up. "I'll introduce you two."

Julie hopped up and held the little girl's hand tightly in hers. "You know … ."

But Michaela was having a hard time containing her excitement and interrupted Julie. "I've been waiting to meet you," exclaimed Michaela, her voice rising to almost a squeal.

"You've been waiting to meet me?" Julie asked tenderly.

"Yep." Michaela took a deep breath and tried to sound grown-up, "Actually, I've been expecting you," Michaela attempted to correct herself.

Julie waited for Michaela to continue, but instead she pulled Julie anxiously as they continued walking. Julie saw that the man was still far in the distance. As they came closer, he stood up and faced them, waiting for them as Michaela had instructed him.

"I told him to wait there," Michaela explained as she smiled up at Julie and gave her the biggest impish smile that Julie had ever seen. And yet, the resemblance of that smile and Michaela's laughter brought a distinct familiarity to Julie's heart.

Michaela slowed down her pace. There was a need for this quiet moment, though Julie wasn't sure why. After a few more steps, Julie spoke softly, "You know, I always loved the name Michaela."

"I know," Michaela answered, letting out a loud giggle. She stopped as they neared the gentleman and turned to face Julie. She tugged on Julie's arm as she had earlier on the man's. She pulled Julie down to her knees and leaned towards her and hugged Julie once again. "I love you," Michaela's small voice echoed into Julie's ears. Julie closed her eyes as their love flowed between them.

Shortly, Michaela slowly began to release her arms from around Julie's neck as she whispered into Julie's ear, "I am going to leave you two alone for just a little while, and then I will come right back."

"But, but ..." Julie started to speak. "But who are ... ?"

Michaela paused and looked directly into Julie's eyes. Heaven's light shone brightly and engulfed them as their souls met, and then Julie knew. She knew immediately, and her eyes were opened. Her heart filled with rapture as she drew Michaela to her side and hugged her tightly once again.

Michaela wiggled free, giggling, and said, "I'll be right back." She turned to go to the man who was approaching them.

"Does he know who you are?" Julie asked.

"He's going to," Michaela giggled as she ran to meet him.

Julie watched as Michaela stopped in front of the man and pulled him down to her side and whispered in his ear. Michaela hugged him tightly and then ran down to the shore. Julie slowly stood up. She was in a kind of daze. This had never happened to her in heaven before. Her heart was so full and she was so distracted that she didn't see the man approach her at first. And then their eyes met. Julie looked deeply into the man's eyes and he into hers. They both paused simultaneously, almost as if in disbelief, and then ran into each other's arms. They knew instantly. They embraced each other and their souls became one. They held each other tightly. The Father's love shone down brightly upon them, embracing them both. Heaven's light beamed ever so brightly.

"We made it," Mike whispered in her ear.

"Together," Julie replied, embracing him once more.

They looked once again into each other's eyes.

"We carried each other," Mike said, as he reached for Julie's hand.

Julie grasped Mike's hand tightly in hers as they began to walk together. "You were my soulmate," Julie whispered softly.

"And you mine," Mike answered, giving her hand a loving squeeze.

They both sat down on the sand as the sound of the waves carried their hearts to a place where they alone were together.

Julie looked at Mike and Mike at her.

Mike asked, "Did you know about Michaela?"

"No," Julie answered. "Not until the Father let her reveal it to me."

"Me neither," Mike continued. "Not until the Father let her reveal it to me."

"I knew she was someone special," Julie remarked.

"Me, too," Mike replied.

"Do you remember miscarrying her," Mike asked.

"I was never sure," Julie answered Mike. "I thought for sure that I was pregnant at that time. I wasn't going to tell anyone until I was sure. I was going to check it out the next day when a car swerved towards me that evening and ran me off the road. That night, the cramps started, and I knew that if I had been pregnant, I had lost the baby. I had always wondered in my heart."

"Our Michaela," Mike added affectionately.

Julie and Mike walked, hand-in-hand, sharing the many victories they had overcome together. Sometimes they spoke, and sometimes there were no words needed. Julie and Mike knew that there was no marriage in heaven. There was a knowledge of this, even when they reunited. Love here was different than love there. Love was not determined or shared by marriage of the past, but by the love that they had shared and that existed for eternity. They shared the joys and love that they alone knew. They looked for sea glass and laughed. The Father joined them and answered the many questions they had. Michaela returned and slipped between them, holding each of their hands as they continued to walk.

Julie turned to the Father, and asked, "Were there others?"

Mike turned to the Father, awaiting his answer.

"By and by, my children. You will understand it better by and by."

And in the essence of that eternal life, they began to understand more of their life's journey and more of the eternal purposes it had served—why Michaela had never been born, if there were others, meeting those who had gone before, greeting those who had followed. And in heaven's light their souls would meet often.

Life Blossoms

chapter

7

One would think that once you were in heaven, you would understand everything. However, the truth is, you are always continually learning. Julie thought about this as she was taking a walk. She loved her walks in the woods. Julie could smell the tantalizing fragrances of heaven. She had learned that some of these were the prayers of the saints who had been collected in golden vials. They would rise in a fine mist and mingle with a sweet savor, perpetuating throughout all of heaven, filling it with a sweet aroma. The mist would sparkle and glitter in heaven's light. There were also vials containing the tears of those who had cried unto God. Julie wondered how different her past world could have been if all of the people there would have realized how powerful the sheer impact of their tears, and the full power of their prayers, could have had on the world.

"They don't always hear us." Julie heard a voice speak to her as she was walking.

"Why?" Julie asked.

The angel answered her question without hesitation. "Because they do not desire to hear us."

Julie loved speaking with the angels. They had such vast knowledge of the past and the present. They knew of the battles each person had fought. They knew of the sacrifices each one had made. They knew because they had been there with us.

Julie continued to walk through the woods. She paused and glanced around. It was here, on one occasion, when she met a few of her angels who had watched over her during her lifetime. To be able to share with these wonderful spiritual beings and receive the knowledge that she truly had never been alone enraptured Julie's heart. Julie kidded with them and remarked, "I actually complained to God one day in prayer about you." The angels smiled at Julie and the Father's presence grew stronger around them. "I asked him if I had worn out all of my guardian angels and did he not have any more to send to help me."

Again, the angels smiled. "The angel of the LORD encamps around about those who fear him, and he delivers them," one replied lovingly. And then he continued, "That day you spoke to the Father, we were there."

"I knew you were!" Julie exclaimed. "I could feel your presence in the room."

"The Father had summoned us to come into his presence to witness that special moment," the angel continued.

"I knew you were there with me in God's presence," Julie spoke slowly, recalling the preciousness of that moment.

"Do you remember what the Father said to you that day?" he asked.

"I do," replied Julie. "I had asked him where he was when my heart had been broken by the life there." And I asked him, "Where were my angels to protect me?"

"And?" the angel gently prodded Julie on.

"And," Julie answered, "he said, 'every time that you cried, the angels cried with you.'"

"And we did," the angel replied lovingly.

Julie continued, "He said, 'every time that you cried, I cried with you.'" The Father joined them at that very moment and covered her once again with his love.

Julie paused from her walk and sat down amidst the flowers. She allowed herself to bathe in his heavenly light. She joined in with the praises that went up before the Lord. The songs arising up throughout heaven mingled with the prayers from below and brought the sweet aroma of praise, which filled the heavenly.

Julie sprung up after a time and continued her walk. She left the garden and meandered through the paths. She passed many precious souls along the way. At times, she would pause and join them and then continue on. Julie turned to the right and walked down a path where she had not traveled before. There she saw a little girl sitting on what appeared to be her mother's lap. The little girl was so precious. Julie wondered why she, herself, was there, because the Father had never let anyone interrupt a reunion. Reunions were moments of sharing that were too precious to allow any interruptions. Julie slowly approached the mother and child. The mother was reading the little girl a book. The little girl giggled as she nestled in her mom's arms. Heaven was so special in this way of bringing loved ones together. Julie loved it. It surpassed all of the theologies she had known that were expressed by man. Words could not express the reality of such a place as this—the beauty, the presence of love, the omnipresence of the Father always surrounding them. No, this truly was heaven.

As she approached the little girl who was sitting upon her mother's lap, Julie would have normally just smiled and walked by as she so often did to passing souls. But everything suddenly changed. As Julie looked at the child, she felt a connection to her, and even in a strange way, to the mother also. Julie began to notice the resemblance of the child. She reminded her some of herself when she was young. The woman gave Julie a warm smile and then faded away.

The little girl then transformed before Julie into a young woman, and then into an older woman whom Julie knew instantly.

"Gramma, it's you!" Julie cried out as she ran to her.

"Julie, it's you!" her gramma cried back.

They ran to each other and embraced. Julie knew instantly at that moment that she was the other of her two grammas. They sat down beneath a beautiful blooming tree and talked.

Here you didn't miss what you didn't know you had. But when you found a soul who you did know, your heart overflowed with joy. It was a joy that could not be felt when she had lived. This joy was iridescent with a love of such intensity that in her past life she would have not been able to contain it in her physical form.

Julie and her gramma stood up from where they were seated and strolled down a path. It led them to a place very similar from their days of old. There was a pavilion with picnic tables. When they sat down, surprisingly, other souls began to meet with them there. Ronnie, Jerry, and Matt joined them along with some of their aunts and uncles and cousins. It reminded Julie of the many family reunions they had all shared so long ago. The songs of old began to float up among them as they began to sing "Beyond the Sunset," "The Old Country Church," and Gramma's favorite, "It Is No Secret".

Such were these beautiful times in this place called heaven. Here nothing was old. Everything was new. Everything was beautiful, and everything was known and revealed, all as the Father knew best.

Jubilees

chapter

8

"The influence of a mother in the lives of her children
is beyond calculation."
~ James E. Faust

One of the most beautiful things about heaven was that it never grew old. Julie continued to learn more and more from the Father, the angels, and the souls who she met. There was much to discover as to what eternity held in store for them. All was unveiled throughout heaven's journey, in increments of knowledge, as the Father would reveal to each individually. Julie had often wondered why there had not been more written about heaven in the Holy Word. But she recalled then, as now, that even with what was written, she had found it hard to fathom: "streets of gold," "walls of jasper," and "gates of pearl." She had believed it when she read it; however, her mortal mind could not understand it then in its fullness, and her mortal mind would not have understood it even now, except that she was in the spiritual. To see things in the spiritual, and to be in the spiritual, made all things now easier to understand.

Julie was so excited, for she had been called with many others to meet a new soul who had now come home. This happened often and was a joyous triumphant time. The angels would sing, and the praises of the saints would rise and mingle with their songs. The gates, all twelve of them, would open wide, and all of heaven would rejoice as the Father's presence would meet another one of his children whom he had called home. At times, souls would linger to greet those who had been closely connected to them. These were great jubilees. But the individual reunions were usually done with the Father in heavenly places.

Julie recalled the moment when she first arrived. She felt a warmth and a knowledge of all the immediate souls who surrounded her. However, her eyes were then only fixed solely upon her Jesus, the Father, whose light drew her into his presence, into his mighty arms of shelter and love, where old things were passed away and behold all things were becoming new.

Julie now anxiously walked to meet this dear soul who had just come home, and joyfully joined with the many others who were gathering for this great homecoming. Julie knew so many of these souls and loved them dearly. As they all came together, their love for each other mingled with the love of the Father and the angels. Praises filled the air, and Julie knew she could never have explained or understood this in her past life.

Even amidst this moment, there were new experiences to enjoy. Julie never knew, even then, when she might meet a soul whom she had not met before. There were souls who were familiar but who had not directly impacted her life. Julie learned that many of these were her ancestors: those who had been born many generations before her and had paved a path for her in the fallen world of her past.

Julie recalled one time when she ran into a woman who truly appeared to be very old. She had pure white hair. Usually, a soul would transition from the recognizable forms that Julie would remember and then settle into the one whom she knew best. She had never before met a soul, who from the beginning remained in one form, and who had snow white hair. Julie smiled at the woman as she started to pass by, but then, as so often would happen, she stopped. The woman smiled warmly at Julie as if she had been waiting for her to come by. Without a word, the kindly old woman took her hand and led Julie to a path where they could be alone in the Father's presence.

"I've been expecting you," the kindly woman said excitedly with a kind smile.

Julie smiled in return and looked into the woman's kind eyes. They were deep blue, blue as where the ocean would meet the sky. Julie felt as if she could swim in the love that the woman's eyes held for her. There was a familiarity in her eyes. Even though Julie recognized them, she couldn't remember the impact that they had had on each other's lives.

"You don't really know me," the woman explained, understanding Julie's bewilderment. "But you are a part of me," she said. She squeezed Julie's hand in affection as they sat down amidst the meadow and talked. It was full of daisies. Julie remembered once seeing a picture of her grandmother in a field of daisies. Julie smiled at the woman. She had her grandmother's eyes. That's what was so familiar.

"I am your great-great-great grandmother," the kindly woman now revealed. "Long before you were born, and long after I had died and come to heaven, God reminded me of a mighty promise he had given me concerning a continual prayer that I had always requested of him. God revealed to me, that it had been fulfilled, even though I didn't get to see it fulfilled in my lifetime."

Julie was caught up in the moment as the Father's presence surrounded them and their love mingled together as one. This was another new experience. Julie hadn't thought about the generational family that had preceded her.

"I had given my heart to God as a little girl," the gentle woman continued. "There were severe hardships that I only know in part. But I refused to leave my faith. I had children and taught them about our Savior who had died for us. But my earnest prayer, one I had always prayed was, "God, my Father, save my children, save my grandchildren, and my great grandchildren, even to all generations."

Julie continued to gaze into this loving woman's eyes. "It was you," Julie spoke softly. "It was you."

The woman looked steadily into Julie's eyes and waited for her to explain.

"I always knew there was someone from my heritage who had laid up a prayer for my soul. Someone who I had never met. I just knew it!" Julie wasn't able to contain the joy of this moment.

They sat and talked and shared. While nurturing Julie in her love, Julie learned much about her family from her lovely great-great-great grandmother.

After a while, the grandmother said to Julie, "I have someone else I want you to meet. She, too, prayed for you all of your life. You will know her and she has been expecting you. She lovingly patted Julie's hand, and then, in a moment, she was gone.

Julie glanced down the path where she had walked with her grandmother and pondered the encounter. She arose and began to walk down the path and let the Father's presence bathe over her soul. Then, in the distance, she saw another person walking towards her along the winding path.

Julie paused and patiently waited. She was now able to see that it was a woman slowly approaching. As Julie continued to watch, the woman came closer and began to walk faster and had a slight lift to her gait. She reminded Julie of her momma, but Julie knew that it wasn't her. Julie stopped and continued to watch the woman as she came nearer. Julie felt slightly puzzled as her heart grew with excitement and anticipation. Julie could feel the Father's love drawing them to each other. Julie reached out her arms to the woman who now had begun to run to her. Julie ran to her too. They embraced and hugged one another. Julie looked into her Aunt Joan's eyes. She knew she would meet her here someday. "Thank you, Auntie," Julie whispered. "Thank you Auntie. You were always there for me. You always prayed for me."

"I love you, Honey," Joanie said in the familiar voice that Julie recognized. Joanie squeezed both of Julie's hands in hers and then embraced her again. They sat down and talked of all the days gone by. Julie's momma soon joined them, and the three of them sat and talked. After a long while, they arose and took each other's hands and walked down the path together.

Ajisth

chapter

9

*"For he shall give his angels charge over you,
to keep you in all your ways."*
~ Psalm 91:11

ulie smiled to herself. She never felt lonely, for truly, she was never alone. Even when she took a walk by herself, heaven's light would always shine down upon her and the Father's presence was always near. She had often wondered in her old life if heaven would be boring with nothing to do, nothing to learn, just floating through the clouds. She still would have preferred that over the anguish of the world that she had left behind. All she knew was when she reached heaven, she was home. She knew somehow that she had fought a good fight. The battle was won and victory was hers. Everything here was always new. You never made plans. Everything just unfolded before you. You could never be bored.

Julie never thought about the Bible having a part in heaven. She had just figured it was God's word for them back then, to lead and keep them in the fallen world. But upon her many visits with the Father, and gatherings together with others at meetings, she realized that what she had known as the Bible was merely a nugget of what was unveiled here. In the past, the Word was representative of what was, what is, and what was to come. But here the Word lived. Here the Word could be felt. "In the beginning was the Word and the Word was with God and the Word was God,"

Julie recalled the scripture of John. "And the Word became flesh and dwelt among us."

Of course, it all made sense, Julie thought. *If the Word was given to us in that life, how could it not exist in this one? If the Word was given there to reveal to us the things that were to come to pass—the Rapture, Tribulation, Armageddon, 1000 years of peace, Satan loosed for a short time, the Great White Throne Judgment, a New Heaven and Earth, and the New Jerusalem—then truly it wouldn't have just been dropped and forgotten here.*

And so it was. Except here, there was full understanding. No more did she have to wonder over the explanations of Daniel and the great Revelation. Julie wondered how anyone could ever think they would be bored in heaven. For here, amidst all the beautiful splendor, the great reunions, the perfect love, the absence of all evil, stood the Word: the Word that had become flesh and dwelt among us, the Word that had come in life and brought promise, the Word that had died on the cross and gave victory over death and hell. There was so much for everyone to learn and understand. For here, the written word was being revealed and coming to pass as it would unfold before them, even as all of heaven prepared for that one and great day that was fast approaching—"the rapture." No one knew when that day would come, not even the angels of heaven. But all of heaven joyfully prepared for that day. Julie had remembered singing the songs of old hundreds of times. "Satan will be bound a thousand years, we'll have no tempter then, after Jesus shall come back to earth again." And one of her ole time favorites, "I'll Fly Away", and also, "I'll See You in the Rapture." No, the Word truly was God, except now, instead of pages in a book, he lived and walked among them, this omnipresent Father, this loving Savior, his presence always shining upon them in heaven's light.

Julie found a new path. As she ran down it, she could hear the rustling of a waterfall far beneath her. Here she sat and pondered these many thoughts. Scurrying down the pathway, she found a perfect place to rest. A rock that was gently worn in the center had made a perfect seat for Julie to sit upon. As she dangled her feet in the water, the light spray of the mist from the falls danced upon her cheeks.

Julie often wondered when all of God's plans would come into play. Before she had passed, the world seemed to have fallen totally from grace. Evil was being called good, and good was being called evil. Many who still believed wondered, even then, how long God would wait to come and call his people home. Many were growing weary. Many had lost their way. Many did not believe and had adopted a form of religion but denied the power thereof.

The thing troubling Julie the most before she left was how much the church had changed. It had changed so subtly that she hadn't even realized it was happening. Slowly, many of the ideals and thoughts of the world and society just crept into the church. If the world said it was right, then it must be right. If man decreed it wasn't really wrong, or declared that people couldn't help it, or that they were just born that way, then the church was supposed to just agree with it. And slowly, ever so gradually, the church began to change. Everyone began to try to find a new way to say things, to be what was called "politically correct," and one was never to dare to offend another. The church became a place simply to come to "feel good." Actually, the world seemed to declare that there must never be any discomfort and had come up with about any pill you could think of, just to enable you to feel good.

Julie had slowly begun to realize then that hell was hardly mentioned anymore. Oh, that was such a dark and dreary place, and it didn't make people feel good. Many would leave the church if it was preached. Besides, many would say, "Who are you to speak of a place such as hell? You're being judgmental." And as truth dried up, and man rose higher, there was less and less of the move of the Spirit of God.

Julie, sat and let her mind wander. Heaven's light shone bright-ly down upon her through the mist as she felt her Father's comfort-ing presence. *How could we have drifted so far from the principles of God?* Julie thought.

"Because the people lost their focus," a voice next to her answered softly.

Julie turned and smiled at the angel who had just joined her. This was the angel whom she loved sitting and talking with the most. She called him, "Ajisth," which means very intelligent, bril-liant, bright, and smart. "I'm so glad you joined me, Ajisth," Julie said smiling. And then on a more serious note asked, "How did we lose our focus, Ajisth?"

"Oh, in so many ways, Julie," Ajisth answered. "Man became comfortable, as in so many generations before him, and began to forget their need for God. They became content in just feeling good and convincing themselves that they weren't really bad, at least not that bad. Their self-content and self-focus along with their denial, minimization, and justification satisfied them. Many still loved God but could not see the need to surrender themselves fully to him. They felt that just saying they loved him was enough."

"But how did we lose the message of the cross, the message of salvation, that there were none good, no not one, the message that we were all sinners?" Julie asked.

"Without the presence of God, man will always lose his way," Ajisth replied.

"Will they find their way again?" Julie asked. "Before the rapture takes place?"

"I believe many will," Ajisth answered. "If they will hunger after the Father, they will."

Julie sat studying the angel as she listened to his words.

"There are many vials of tears and prayers that still are continu-ing to fill for these lost souls," he continued. "If my people, which are called by my name, shall humble themselves, pray, and seek my face, and turn from their wicked ways, then I will hear from heaven, and will forgive their sins, and will heal their land," Ajisth quoted the Word.

Julie smiled. "Then there's still a chance of many more coming."

"Many more," Ajisth smiled. "God's ear does not grow so heavy that he does not hear, and his arm is not short that he cannot save."

As Julie sat and continued to talk with Ajisth, she learned he had been very much involved in her life. He had been appointed and sent many times by the Father to go to her aid, to warn her, and to encourage her.

"Heaven is such a wonderful place," Julie remarked happily. "I wish those living below could know this."

"They can know, Julie," Ajisth responded, giving Julie a smile. "When man enters into God's presence and asks him to come into their hearts and to fill them with his presence; and when they dare to confess that outside of all their proposed goodness, that in their heart, they are still yet sinners; when they ask God to forgive and wash away their sins, and acknowledge that he is the Christ, the Savior, who died for their sins, then they will experience the "essence" of heaven. They can never believe in this heaven, and that it is real, if they cannot believe in a Jesus who died just for them."

Julie slowly nodded in agreement. She could feel the Father's presence build around them. Others had begun to join them now and were listening. They began to ask Ajisth questions as more of the angels gathered with them. Songs began to rise up in praise and heaven's light shone brighter as God embraced them in his presence.

Julie wondered if she was ever given the chance, how she could ever write words to describe this. *How does one paint a picture in three dimensions? How does one tell a story when there are no words to describe it?*

Ajisth looked at Julie and lovingly smiled. Julie could see that he radiated with the Father's presence. "Eye cannot see, and ear cannot hear, neither has entered into the heart of man, the things which God has prepared for them that love him," Ajisth reminded Julie.

A Strange Encounter

chapter

10

*"What we do for ourselves dies with us.
What we do for others and the world
remains and is immortal."*
~ Albert Pine

Heaven remained busy making great preparations for all of the heavenly events that were soon to come to pass. Julie felt such joy and anticipation. New souls continually joined them. There were great times of jubilees, reunions, and many gatherings about the things that were yet to come to pass. Amidst all of the celebrations and preparations, Julie loved the jubilees. The times of jubilee were probably some of the grandest times that Julie enjoyed in heaven. The trumpets would sound, and many would feel the call to gather for the rejoicing and welcoming of another soul who had come home. Often, she knew some of these souls, yet, there were so many that she did not know. The wonderful thing was knowing that somehow they were a part of you. Here, everyone was bonded together as one by the Father's love and presence. Julie loved listening to the wonderful stories of how each soul had overcome. It reminded her of the old song she used to sing, *"We will tell the story, how we've overcome, and we'll understand it better by and by."*

Julie began to walk down a wide pathway. At first, it was busy with many souls. Julie continued to walk aimlessly. She had just come from one of the great jubilees and her heart was overflowing.

67

The path began to narrow and Julie needed to decide whether to go right or left. The pathway to the left seemed less traveled and Julie chose this one. As she walked, her surroundings became more colorful. There was what appeared to be a cherry tree to the right of the road. She stopped, walked over to the tree, and sat down under it. As she sat there, several souls periodically walked past and they warmly greeted each other. Others, would sometimes stop and sit down and talk with her. After a while, Julie thought about walking back the way she had come. However, there was one more soul approaching her, and she thought she'd linger for just a little while longer.

As the soul approached, once again she began to feel the familiarity of knowing this person. Somehow, Julie knew they had met before, but sensed that this was not exactly a reunion. Yet still, she watched with joyful anticipation to greet him.

She then realized who it was, at least in part. It was the soul whom she had talked about with the Father earlier in the garden. Julie wondered if she might gain a better knowledge of him. Maybe this is why the Father had led her down this path. She wasn't afraid of him. There was nothing to fear in heaven for there was no evil there. Julie could feel the presence of the Father gather around her strongly. She always felt strengthened and fortified in his presence. Julie wondered if Ajisth would join her but thought he probably would not. She had learned that during times of growth and gaining more knowledge, or at times of revelation and lessons that her Father wanted to intimately teach her, she would always be alone with the person while being surrounded by the Father's immense presence.

Julie continued to sit and watched the man slowly approach. She crisscrossed her legs like she had when she was a child, and just waited. As the man drew nearer he stopped and smiled at Julie. It was a kind smile, as all the smiles were from the souls who were here. But this one was more pronounced. She gazed into his eyes and instantly knew there was a knowledge of an impact upon their lives, but there was no revelation of what that knowledge was. The man looked deeply into Julie's eyes. Never in all the souls who Julie had encountered in heaven had any one's eyes been so full of thankfulness. *That's what was different about this soul,* Julie thought. *It wasn't just that he was familiar and that somehow they were connected from their past, but it was that expression of devout thankfulness that radiated in his eyes.*

Julie smiled in return and thought that the man would probably pass by as he had before. However, this time, he stopped. He paused as if he wasn't sure whether he should stop or pass by. Julie waited in the Father's presence. Somehow, she thought this soul needed a time of pause for himself, as much as Julie also needed it. Julie knew the Father would have it unfold according to his plan.

The man looked at Julie, but he could see what Julie could not see. He saw the presence of the Father covering her, and he saw her transform before him as he had known her in their past. He, too, waited for the Father to guide him. He had spoken to the Father many times about Julie, and the Father had told him that he would lead him and give him knowledge to all things in his time.

"Your name is Julie," the man spoke for the first time.

"Yes," Julie answered softly. Though puzzled, she waited. Heaven's light shone down upon her as if in a direct beam of light radiating throughout her whole being. Julie had never felt such power and love. It comforted her in a way unlike any that she had experienced here in heaven.

Julie waited for him to possibly mention his name, but he didn't utter a word.

The man finally managed to say, "There is much I would like to share with you." He paused and then continued, "But the Father has said that it will happen at a later time."

There was something familiar about the man, Julie thought, *something in his eyes and the sound of his voice.* Julie recognized it in part, but it was too different from the voice of her past, and she wasn't able to ascertain the knowledge of their two lives. This didn't trouble Julie, but it did cause her to wonder about the man and their situation.

"It's because you never knew me in my redeemed state," the man stated kindly to Julie. "That's why you don't know me."

Julie could only nod at the man in understanding. For some reason, she truly had no desire to inquire of the man or ask him any questions. She thought it best just to listen to him.

"I knew you in your redeemed state," he continued. "That's why I can recognize you."

Julie stood staring at the man and waited for him to continue. However, he just smiled at her kindly as he nodded and told her good-bye.

"Good-bye," Julie said slowly. She watched the man walk past her and down the path. She stretched out her legs and laid back to rest under the broad cherry tree. Julie let her soul pour out to her Savior all that she felt. She rested in his presence, a still and peaceful rest. She felt a soft warm breeze blow over her as heaven's light glimmered down upon her. *By and by,* she thought. *She would understand it all better, by and by.*

Heavenly Reunions

chapter

11

> *"A friend is someone who understands your past,*
> *believes in your future,*
> *and accepts you just the way you are."*
> ~ Unknown

Julie ran down the trail, laughing as she went. She felt like a kid again. "Will you please wait up?" came a voice from behind her. Julie only giggled and continued running.

She was on her way to one of her favorite places, the waterfall. She sat down upon the rock where she always sat whenever she came here. Her friend, emerging from the bushes which hid the trail, joined Julie. Julie watched her friend's eyes widen at the sight of the waterfall.

"Have you ever been here?" Julie asked.

"No," her friend slowly replied, totally mesmerized by the waterfall.

"It's my secret place," Julie remarked. "I couldn't wait to bring you here. I remember how much we used to love to sit by rustling water and talk to each other."

Julie allowed her friend to stand and gaze at the waterfalls without interrupting her. She watched as the water splashed onto her face and dampened her hair. Julie had just found her best friend and wanted to share everything with her as they had in their past lives. Julie remembered Pam instantly when they met at one of the jubilees and homecoming. When their eyes met, it was as if they had never parted.

Pam came over and sat by her little friend. They had been friends for over sixty years, until one day Pam passed away unexpectedly. It had crushed Julie to lose this dear friend who was more like a sister.

"I've been expecting you," Pam remarked as she reached out and took Julie's hand into hers.

Julie felt her friend's soft pudgy hands clasp around hers, these hands that had often given Julie a comforting touch. Julie squeezed them tightly. She loved how she could see her loved ones as she had known them before, except now they were whole. There were no wrinkles of age, or scars, or weariness etched onto their faces. There was no pain radiating from their eyes or anguish in their voices. There were no handicaps, or sickness, or blindness, or diseases. Everyone was whole and in their perfect state.

Julie gazed at Pam as they continued to hold each other's hands. "I hadn't noticed," Julie exclaimed. "I hadn't noticed it was gone."

"What's gone?" Pam asked laughing.

"The birthmark on your face above your eye," Julie remarked as she touched Pam's face where it used to be.

"I know," Pam replied smiling. "All my pains are gone, Julie—no more depression, no more sorrow, no more loneliness."

Julie just sat and stared at Pam, and Pam at *her Julie*. "I wanted to bring you here for our special reunion," Julie continued.

"I love it, Julie," Pam replied softly with a smile.

"I knew you would," Julie nodded.

"You were always crazy about waterfalls and the ocean," Pam reflected as she let her feet drop into the water beside Julie's. They sat dangling their feet as heaven's light and God's omnipresent love flowed over them.

"You always loved them too," Julie spoke softly, as she continued to look ahead into the falls. Pam smiled and then turned to Julie.

"You were very upset when I passed," Pam spoke openly.

"I was," Julie replied back to her friend.

"I had to come home, Julie. I just had to," Pam explained. "I had no more fight left in me."

Julie smiled. "I know, Pam. I really did understand. But I was angry at you for a while. I used to tell God that it wasn't right. It wasn't supposed to be that way. I told him that you and I were going to grow old together, sit in rocking chairs, and turn the nursing home upside down."

Pam laughed. "Yes, we were going to do that. But I could bear no more Julie. I had to come home."

"I know," Julie added in a low whisper. "I knew it then. I just missed you so much, our talks, our venting sessions, and our love."

"I remember that last day at the hospital, before I crossed over," Pam remarked looking steadily into her friend's eyes.

"But how could you?" Julie asked. "You were pretty much catatonic by the time I got there."

"I remember everyone who was there," Pam added. "I remember every word spoken, every tear that fell. And I remember every word that you spoke to me, Julie."

Julie's eyes focused upon her dear friend and studied her. "I knew I had to let you go."

"You told me, 'You fought the fight. You kept the faith, Pammy. There is a crown waiting for you.'" Pam shifted in her position and reached out and took Julie's hand. "You stayed and stroked my head until my last breath was gone. I watched you as I departed."

"I knew how important it was for you to feel touch," Julie expressed tenderly. "You had suffered so much loneliness. I just wanted you to know we were all there for you. I wanted you to feel our presence before you passed."

"I did, Julie. I truly did. I could see everyone who was in the room." Pam paused and then continued, "Did you feel and see the angels in the room that day?"

"No," Julie answered, surprised at her friend's remark.

"I thought you might have," Pam continued, with excitement rising in her voice. "They surrounded us in that room, singing their beautiful songs, and ushered in the presence of our Father."

Julie smiled at the revelation that her friend had shared. She squeezed her friend's hand and began to stand up. "Oh, let's sit a little longer," Pam pressed. Julie looked into her friend's eyes. She couldn't help seeing that familiar twinkle that she remembered when they were kids.

"I thought I'd join you," came a familiar voice from the woods where the trail opened up to the falls.

Julie jumped up as Pam followed, smiling from ear to ear.

"Vicki, it's you," Julie called out.

"Hi, Julie!" Vicki exclaimed. "I've been expecting you." She reached out her arms and embraced Julie tightly.

Julie and Vicki then turned and faced Pam, drawing her into their embrace.

"Together again," Julie whispered softly.

"Together again," Pam and Vicki echoed back.

"Friends for a lifetime," Julie added.

"Sisters forever," Pam and Vicki finished Julie's quote from their past.

Julie stared at the two sisters who had been her dearest friends throughout her whole life and then started to laugh. "What?" Pam asked with a sly twinkle in her eye like Julie had seen earlier.

"I knew it. I just knew you were up to something," Julie laughed looking at Pam and then Vicki. Vicki smiled back at Julie with that same twinkle in her eye.

"I remember seeing that same look in both of your eyes when you brought me home to my surprise sixteenth birthday party—my first ever birthday party."

"We both wanted to surprise you," Vicki and Pam sounded in unison, laughing.

They then walked toward the falls, and all three of them sat down together. They talked, shared, and reminisced. They laughed and kidded each other and recalled the many happy days gone by.

Memories

chapter

12

"A man's very highest moment is,
I have no doubt at all,
when he kneels in the dust and beats his breast
and tells all the sins of his life."
~ Oscar Wilde

Julie concentrated on her thoughts as she walked along a path leading to the garden where she would meet with the Father. Julie had always had a strong memory. It was one of the gifts the Father had given her in that life. She thought in her finite mind that when someone came to heaven, they would have no memories of their past. But, Julie marveled, that here in heaven, she had so many precious memories filling her with joy.

But how could we not remember? Julie thought. *If we had no memory, then we would cease to be who we were. We would lose our identity and our personality. It would be as if a part of our soul was erased.*

Julie thought of how God, in his infinite wisdom, created the spiritual being to be spirit and soul, and how each spirit and soul could know, and have knowledge, without the sorrow and pain. Even if the knowledge was in increments, it was an absolute truth because it was pure truth being revealed in the Father's light. Here there was no perception of truth as in the past, where man would create what he deemed to be a truth by his own definition and conception; a created truth to justify and satisfy his own state of mind; a truth he could believe in to assuage his own doubt, his fears and shame, his guilt and blame; a truth that could change from day to day to fit every need or occasion of life; a truth that in reality was a lie.

Julie thought deeply about the story of Lazarus and the rich man in the Bible. She remembered how both of them had known each other in their mortal lives and how both had died. *But both of their lives were different,* Julie mused. In his past life, Lazarus was poor, hungry and covered with sores, but he loved and believed in God. The rich man, however, was clothed in purple and fine linen and ate sumptuously every day and didn't serve God. Both died. Lazarus was carried away by angels into the bosom of Abraham. The rich man just died and was buried. When both entered eternity, the rich man found himself in hell and in torment, wherein, he was able to see Lazarus in the bosom of Abraham.

Julie let her thoughts continue. The rich man cried out and said, "Father Abraham, have mercy on me, and send Lazarus, that he may dip the tip of his finger in water and cool my tongue, for I am tormented in this flame."

Abraham responded to the rich man, "Son, remember that you in your lifetime received good things, and likewise Lazarus received evil things: but now he is comforted, and you are tormented."

Julie thought to herself how it was interesting that angels had come for Lazarus, but the rich man had just died and then was buried. She also couldn't get over the nerve of the rich man asking Lazarus, of all people, to bring him a drink of water—Lazarus, the man whom he had rejected the most. But what was more intriguing to Julie was that Father Abraham continued to relay the depth of the current situation to the rich man saying, "And besides all of this, there is a great gulf fixed between us and you, so that they which would pass from here to you, cannot; neither can they pass to us, that would come from there."

It would have been enough for Abraham just to give this one reason alone to the rich man and to have left his answer at that. But for some reason it was important for Abraham, and all who read this, to know that even if there was no gulf between them, he wanted the rich man to *remember* how Lazarus had been treated. And then, not only did the rich man remember this, but he also *remembered* that he had five brothers yet in his past. He then asks Abraham to send Lazarus back to them, and to testify to them, so that they would not come to this place of torment. He believed that if someone would come back from the dead, maybe his brothers would then believe. But Abraham reminded the rich man that they had Moses and the prophets. And if they would not listen to them, they surely would not listen to a poor ragged beggar who used to sit at their gates, even if he did come back from the dead.

Julie neared the garden. Oh, how she loved it here. She looked up and saw heaven's light surrounding her. She smiled as she entered the gates to the garden and skipped down the lane until she arrived at her favorite sitting place. Julie sat there, taking everything in: the sounds, the aromas, the beauty, and most of all, the presence of God, which radiated throughout all of heaven and shone down so brightly in heaven's light. Julie rested, knowing that soon the Father would join her.

Once again, she fell into deep thought. *How dare that rich man ask anything of Lazarus?* And the thing that bothered Julie the most was that the rich man never even addressed Lazarus.

He still treats Lazarus as if he was valueless, Julie thought. *As if Lazarus was still the rich man's servant. Instead of addressing Lazarus, he talks to Father Abraham as if Lazarus was not even in their midst. He never speaks or even acknowledges Lazarus. And never, not once, does he show any remorse—not to Lazarus, and not to Father Abraham, for all the evil that he had done.* Julie marveled, *how could the rich man still have no Godly sorrow, or repentance, not even in hell?*

Julie turned and stretched out her legs and rested her back on the trunk of a tree. This was probably her favorite tree in all of heaven. The trunk was moss-covered, soft as velvet. When Julie would rub up against its soft fine fibers, a sweet aroma would be released flowing up and encircling Julie. It tickled her nose and filled the air with its beautiful fragrance.

Julie was thankful for all of her memories. She loved sitting and sharing them with her family and friends, with Ajisth and the other angels, and even the Father.

Julie's mind drifted to another subject that she hoped the Father would help her understand better as he had helped her to understand so many of the other mysteries of the ages and of heaven itself. She began to wonder and ponder over the meeting that she had had with the man who had known her name. She continued to hear his voice echo in her mind, over and over again. Its familiarity rang in her ears and yet she could not connect with him.

Julie thought of other souls who she had met in heaven where she had felt a similar experience. However, though they had an impact on her also, as this man had, they too were not clearly known as she had known her family and others who were close to her.

The one thing all of these souls had in common was that she had only known them in their "unredeemed nature," while they had known her in her "redeemed state." That's how they could recognize her, yet she was not able to recognize them until the Father would reveal their connection to her.

Julie realized what this meant was that when she had known them on earth, they had not yet given their heart to God, or repented of their sins. But when they knew her, she had already given her heart to God, so they would see her as she was. However, when Julie would see them now, they did not appear the same as she would have known or remembered them from her past. Their sins had since been forgiven. Old things were passed away, and they had become new creatures in Christ. So the familiarity was there, but not the connection.

When you looked at a redeemed soul, they did not appear as the same person who you knew back then before they had given their life to Christ. It's amazing what a mean, contrary, backbiting, and bitter person looks like after they have been redeemed. They no longer look like the same person. You don't see their sin, feel their attitude, disdain, or hatred. All of these characteristics are etched into the person and become a part of who they are. But when they are redeemed, all of these features are gone, changed. The person is no longer the same, nor do they appear the same.

Julie recollected the first time she had truly recognized Lindsey, her old classmate from when she was a child. Julie had seen her at various times throughout heaven. Each time they had met, the impact became a little more complete. Julie had long ago forgiven Lindsey from the bullying and heartache that she had caused her as a child. There was no sorrow or pain in the memory because God had taken this pain from Julie when she had long ago forgiven her. But Julie would have never recognized Lindsey's soul in heaven because the person she had known then was mean and evil. Lindsey no longer appeared as that same person after she had been forgiven. So when Julie met her in heaven, it had taken quite a few encounters before Julie was able to have knowledge of their connection.

Julie talked to the Father about all of this many times while resting in his presence. He had told her that by and by she would understand all things. He once explained to Julie, "Had these souls not given their hearts to me, and been redeemed, Julie would have never met them in heaven, for they would have, by their own choice, gone to hell and never been saved."

And there was that word again, *hell*. Julie thought how people had hated the mention of the word, *hell*. People had often said to her, "What kind of loving God would send people to an everlasting hell of fire so bad and so full of pain that it would cause those who were there to gnash their teeth? That's not a loving God."

Julie had tried to explain to them, "Hell was never made for mankind to go there. Hell was created solely for the angels that had rebelled with Lucifer against God and for Lucifer, that great fallen angel, that great prince, angel of angels, who was cast out of heaven for his rebellion, and for trying to overthrow God and his kingdom."

They would try to push her words aside. "But," Julie would plead for them to listen, "don't you see, Lucifer took one-third of the angels with him when he went. Then and only then was hell created. It was never meant for mankind."

Julie meditated upon these thoughts once again as she sat and felt the gentle heavenly breezes brush past her. How sad it was to read in the Bible how Satan had beguiled Eve with his lies and temptations. And how in turn, Eve had turned and beguiled Adam with the same lies and temptations. Julie shifted once again to get comfortable. *They chose to sin,* Julie thought sadly. Their choice brought mankind from their perfect world into a fallen and sinful world. A world where redemption could not be given for that sin or any other sin until Jesus had become the great lamb of sacrifice and died for all of us. Until his death, only sin offerings could be offered for their sins. But these offerings could only cover their sins, not redeem them from their sins. It took God's own blood to redeem his children, to all who would heed his call.

Julie's heart thought about how powerful and dangerous was the gift that God had given mankind—the "power of choice." And yet it was necessary for man to be able to choose.

But how would they choose? Julie wondered. The Bible tells us, "… because of the sins of men, hell has enlarged itself."

"We choose the path of sin, and we choose to go to hell. God does not send us there; we choose where we want to go," Julie softly spoke to herself.

But many who she had shared this with would only scoff and doubted the existence of a place called hell. Some, in rejecting hell, also scoffed at the idea of any such place as heaven. *There is a heaven to gain and a hell to shun,* Julie thought, again remembering the scriptures.

Julie could hear the angels singing and the praises of the souls joining them. These were songs not just from the souls who were here in heaven, but also the songs of those who were still living below. Julie knew the Father would join her soon. He was always in their midst. His presence was never far. Julie closed her eyes and let heaven's light shine down upon her and bathe her with the warmth of his presence and love. She allowed the music, this heavenly chorus that filled the air, to bless her soul. *Redeemed,* Julie thought, and then voiced the word aloud, "Redeemed." *What a special word. It brought to remembrance a song that she had sung as a child in the old country church.* "Redeemed, Redeemed, Redeemed by the blood of the Lamb. Redeemed, Redeemed, his child and forever I am."

"Each Soul Matters"

chapter
13

*"Every single human soul has more meaning and value
than the whole of history."*
~ Nikolai A. Berdyaev

The Father joined Julie in the beautiful garden. Julie poured everything out from her heart unto him. She asked him question after question on all the things she had ever pondered.

It was difficult to explain the enlightenment that she had gained on all of her thoughts, just by being in God's presence. Words were not needed in heaven. Thoughts did not have to process through a finite human mind as in her past. These things could never have been understood on earth. Here, God's presence was so real, so true, that it brought a revelation and understanding to all things. On earth, words from a finite mind would try to express the essence of what was thought to be true. Words which filtered through mortal minds, would try to understand and express a spiritual realm. However, here, there were no mortal filters, just our spirits and souls. Here the spiritual understood the spiritual.

"Do you understand, Julie?" her Father asked.

"I do," Julie answered back, as she sat engulfed in the presence of her heavenly Father. She closed her eyes allowing his presence to carry her.

Slowly, she spoke again, "I wish everyone could experience heaven."

"Everyone?" Father asked.

"Oh, yes," Julie answered without a second thought. "Heaven is more than any person could ever perceive. Even in the spiritual, it is more than any person could ever put into mortal words."

"I go to prepare a place for you," Father interjected softly. "If it were not true, I would have told you so."

"There are many mansions here," Julie continued. She sat up and turned to the Father. "Have I seen them all?" Julie asked inquisitively.

The Father looked down into Julie's eyes letting her look deeply into his, and he did not say a word.

Julie felt as one with her Savior, wrapped in her Father's love. "There are many mansions here," she whispered, as she continued to look into his eyes. "Many mansions," she echoed quietly once again, "all so different."

"I go to prepare a place for you," Father repeated.

"A different place for each of us?" Julie asked.

"A different place for each, and yet together," he answered smiling. "The biggest stumbling block that I find," he continued, and then paused.

Julie was mystified. "Can there be a stumbling block?" she asked.

"Yes," he replied sadly, "my children do not know that they matter."

Julie was puzzled. *Surely we do*, she thought tentatively, curious at the Father's words.

"You think you do," Father continued, as if reading Julie's mind. "But you really cannot grasp the fullness of my love."

"Calvary taught us this," Julie interjected.

"It taught you that I love mankind," Father smiled down at Julie while she rested in his embrace. "But you could not understand that I loved you individually. That for just one of you, I would have died."

"So, each one of us really mean that much to you?"

"Yes."

"I think we got a glimpse of that love when we felt your presence," Julie continued, freely speaking from her heart.

"A glimpse," Father acknowledged as he smiled again at Julie.

"Tell me more," Julie asked. "I understand, but I like to hear you explain it to me."

"Every soul is of unprecedented value. Each soul was created specifically by me. Divine life and spirit were breathed into each one of you upon creation," he continued.

"But why are we not aware of it there?" Julie asked. "Most don't know this, or only in part. It's more of a wish that they would matter to someone, anyone, more than it is ever a reality."

"They are consumed almost from birth to be someone," Father answered softly, yet earnestly. "They deem their value on their looks, their gifts, their station of life, their family, their wealth, their social status. They spend their lifetime searching for their identity, for wealth, or fame. Ever seeking, but never finding their place in life, nor finding their true identity and purpose."

Julie let the Father's words and presence flow over her. She could feel all of heaven surrounding her. She could hear the sounds of heaven, the praises, and the music. The sweet aroma of praise rose and hung in the air.

"These truths are only discovered through the great mysteries of God," said a familiar voice.

Julie turned to see Ajisth, who had joined them. She smiled. She loved when Ajisth would join them in these discussions. She had learned that the Father would often summon him to join them.

"People do not seek God in these matters," Ajisth continued.

"When I first created Adam and Eve, I knew them," Father continued to explain.

"Jeremiah said, 'before you were in your mother's womb, I knew you,'" Julie quoted the words softly.

"I marveled that it was all good," Father continued; "the garden, the beauty, the animals, all creatures great and small."

There was a quiet, a period of pure peace. Julie closed her eyes, enjoying this special moment. Suddenly, she stirred, and then sitting up quickly, turned to Ajisth and then God. Ajisth and God looked at each other and smiled.

"What?" Julie asked.

"Go ahead and ask us," Ajisth said with a slight chuckle.

Julie smiled at both of them. She knew, that they knew, what she was going to ask them. "Are there animals here?" Julie asked.

The Father nodded to Ajisth to answer her.

Ajisth smiled and answered, "We did not say there were."

"But there will be animals in the *New Jerusalem*, right?" Julie asked. "The wolf also shall dwell with the lamb, and the leopard shall lie down with the kid; and the calf and the young lion and the fatling together; and a little child shall lead them," Julie continued.

"Yes," Ajisth answered smiling, "there will be animals in the *New Jerusalem*".

"So, are there no animals, here?" Julie prodded.

The Father winked at Ajisth and then smiled at Julie. "We did not say there weren't."

Julie smiled back at the two of them. She knew that this was her answer.

The Father turned to her once more. "So you said earlier, Julie, that you wished everyone could come to heaven?"

"Yes, I really do!" Julie exclaimed.

"Everyone?" Father asked her on a more serious note.

"Well, I know that no one can come here who have not chosen to come. And I would never want anyone evil to come here," Julie continued. "It would cease to be heaven if evil could come here."

"That is true, Julie," Ajisth replied.

"So not everyone?" Father asked.

Julie searched Father's face and also Ajisth's, and then asked, "But if they've been redeemed from the evil … ."

"If they've been redeemed," Ajisth interjected, and then asked Julie, "What about those who transgressed against others, but then truly repented and sought God for forgiveness?"

"Well, surely they would be in heaven," Julie replied.

"How will they both live in heaven?" Father asked Julie. "The offender and the offended?"

"It's because of *forgiveness*," Julie spoke openly from her heart.

"Yes, because of *forgiveness*," Ajisth repeated.

"But not only my forgiveness," Father replied.

"No, because the one who was hurt must forgive also," Julie added. "When we are hurt by someone, we have to give that hurt and pain to you. And you take it away and heal our hearts. And then, and only then," Julie said emphatically, "we are able to forgive them."

"But would you expect to meet them here?" Father sincerely asked Julie.

"If they have been redeemed from their sins, then surely they would be here," Julie answered searching Father's face once again.

"But would you expect to meet them here?" Father persisted in questioning Julie.

"There is no sorrow here," Julie said attentively.

"You are right, Julie. When one gives me their hurt and pain, I do take it from them. I heal the broken heart. I make them a new creature who is whole and complete."

"And you do the same for all of us when we repent," Julie added. "You make all of us a new creature in Christ. For all have sinned and come short of the glory of God."

"All have sinned and come short of the glory of God," Ajisth repeated, emphasizing Julie's words.

Julie reflected upon their conversation. She knew the Father was teaching her something and she wanted to grasp all of it. Shortly, Julie remarked, "I do remember, when I met Lindsey here and many others who were like her. It took a while for me to recognize them. But they had all recognized me."

"These were those who had offended and hurt you, Julie," her Father explained. "They knew you because you had forgiven them. But you did not know them at first. They were familiar, but you could not connect with them because they appeared differently in their redeemed state than you had known them in their sinful state," God explained once again to Julie. He had explained this to her before, but each time, Julie came to have a better understanding and knowledge of the mysteries and joys of heaven.

Julie reflected over their conversation, "Every soul really does matter," Julie softly spoke the words as if they were as fragile as glass.

"Every soul matters," Ajisth repeated and smiled at Julie.

"All who have fallen, all who have sinned, all who have turned away from their own works, failures, and shortcomings," Julie said. And then she added, "All those who wanted to be redeemed. They all matter."

"I carefully created and formed every soul with their own identity and for a purpose. A purpose not just for me," God said, "but for their own realization that they are a *King's Child*. All of you were created in my image, transformed in body, soul, and spirit."

"But no one seems to understand this on earth," Julie earnestly expressed her heart. "Surely if they truly knew this, they would forsake all things."

"But," Ajisth interjected. "They do not seek to know this. Instead, they continually try to fill the gap and void of their souls with anything and everything that they can."

"Why?" Julie inquired earnestly. "Why is God the last thing on their minds?"

"Because man has transposed God into a religion. A religion that casts God as an image more than a reality. An image of a God, who is an old man, carrying a rod, eager to correct those who fall from his graces," Ajisth continued.

"But how can they not feel his love?" Julie asked.

"Because they have not sought that love," Ajisth stirred as he spoke passionately. "They seek to fulfill their own needs and their own wants. They create their own identity, and vary it to fulfill their own desires, lusts, and pride of life. They seek to establish this in their own might and power rather than seek the one who created them. They do anything, rather than surrender their own will, and humbly find the love of a Father who desires nothing but their redemption and happiness."

"I wish they could know the Savior's love," Julie pressed. "That's what drew me to you."

The Father, who had been sitting quietly and listening to Ajisth and Julie talk, turned to Julie and smiled. He looked directly into her eyes, his love flowing into her soul.

"It was that love that led me to you. It was that presence of love that drew me, and drew me to your heart—past my will, my failures, man's religion, and my own sinful nature," Julie softly explained.

"It was his love," Ajisth reiterated.

"It was his love and his presence. It was his unconditional love that continually persevered and pursued after my soul, revealing the reality of a God who truly did love me; the reality of a God, to whom I truly did matter." Julie sat quietly and reflected upon their conversation as Ajisth and she paused for a moment. There was a solace and a peace that passed human understanding as they abode in the Father's presence.

After a while, the Father's voice broke the silence. His voice was so tender and soft. "Satan has desired to sift my children as wheat. But I have prayed for them. He has sought from their birth to steal, kill, and destroy. But I came to give them life and to give them life more abundantly. His only desire has been to take them out of my hand. But he cannot because every one of them are carved deep into the palm of my hand. Not that he has any concern for them, but that he wants to try to take from me what is rightfully mine. They were never his to take. By my stripes, before Calvary, they were healed. By my blood, on Calvary, they were redeemed. And even in death, I conquered the grave and took back the keys of death and hell. For the gates of hell can no longer prevail against them."

"But, they must choose," Julie said passionately.

"Oh, that power of choice, that each soul alone must choose and work out his own salvation," Ajisth stated.

"Choose you this day, who you will serve," Julie quoted the Word. "Whether it be God or mammon."

"It is grace," Ajisth softly continued.

"It is *amazing grace*," Julie repeated with a smile.

The sounds of heaven began to rise in melodious harmony. The Father took Julie's hand as they began to walk down the path. Ajisth followed beside them.

"Ajisth has something I want him to show you." The Father smiled at Julie.

Julie smiled back as the Father's presence hovered near, never parting, as the heavenly light shone brightly. Its brilliant rays streamed down over them, covering Julie and Ajisth with God's glory, and causing Julie's face to radiate with the Father's love.

Ajisth reached out and took Julie's hand as they walked down a path lit by a single ray of heaven's light.

"Each soul matters," Julie repeated the words softly, her heart overflowing with love.

"Each soul matters," Ajisth repeated, giving Julie a big smile.

"Children's Gate"

chapter

14

"But Jesus said,
'Suffer the little children, and forbid them not,
to come unto me: for of such is the kingdom of heaven.'"
~ Matthew 19:14

There was no darkness in heaven for the light of God radiated throughout. It seemed to pulsate and brighten at the mention of his name ... *Jesus, Emmanuel ... God with us*, shining down upon the twelve pearly gates of heaven, causing them to be iridescent—reflecting beautiful dancing rainbows as you walked through them.

Julie walked down the path with Ajisth and admired the beauty of heaven's light shimmering before them. It reminded her of a beautiful scene that she remembered from her past. Julie began to describe it to Ajisth as they walked. "The sun would shine ever so brightly, Ajisth. You could hardly look into its brightness. Then out of nowhere, clouds would begin to creep in and pass over in front of the sun. Everything would grow dim for just a second or two, and then with no warning, bright shining rays would pierce through the darkness, as arrows of light, dispersing a path from heaven's shore to mankind."

Ajisth smiled as Julie continued to reflect. "I'd sit, mesmerized by its brightness, and peer into the sky with its heavenly display of beauty. I used to call it, *'stairways to heaven.'"*

"You almost felt as if you could race up the translucent beams of light and enter into heaven's gate, didn't you?" Ajisth asked Julie as they continued down the winding path.

"How did you know?" Julie asked.

"I was with you," Ajisth reminded her.

Julie smiled a broad smile. "But there is no comparison to this," Julie added. "Nothing can compare to heaven's light."

"Because the light here is his presence," Ajisth added.

"Rays from the Father's presence, lighting pathways throughout all of heaven," Julie added.

Julie continued to walk with Ajisth at her side, soaking in all of heaven's beauty. The music of heaven's chorus filled the air and seemed to carry Julie to where they were headed.

"Oh the beautiful mysteries of heaven," Julie said softly. Julie knew now that she could never see all of heaven. Every scene was new, fresh, and alive; she was forever meeting new souls, telling the stories of all they had shared, and understanding it all better each day.

Julie and Ajisth walked slowly down the many never-ending paths. Julie stopped often to share with the precious souls who she met along the way. They were in no hurry. Time was nonsensical. It did not exist here. It was not needed. All was ever-present.

The path on which they were now walking narrowed, forming a single pathway. In the distance there appeared to be what reminded Julie of a large mountain. Heaven's light beamed brightly before her. As it touched upon the streets of gold, it cast prisms which seemed to dance upon the surface. Julie walked with great anticipation. Her soul sensed that a great mystery awaited her. The further she walked, the closer she came to that great source of light and the Father's presence. Julie could feel the warmth of his love radiating down upon her.

Ajisth walked quietly by her side, allowing Julie to experience the beauty as it unfolded before her. Julie had never visited this part of heaven. The path began to wind slowly uphill through a dense forest. As she entered into the forest, the air mingled with the many fragrances that permeated throughout the gardens creating an ambrosial aroma saturating Julie's senses. Julie took a deep breath and felt, more than smelled, its sweet fragrance.

The music, the smell, the beauty, and heaven's light engulfed and filled Julie with their essence. Julie could feel the Father's presence as always, but it was more intense, more powerful, and more serene than she had ever felt it. This was a different experience. Often she would feel the Father's presence as a Father, or sometimes as a Savior. But today it was different.

She turned to Ajisth and smiled. He took her hand and led her over to a grassy knoll where they sat down. Julie leaned her back against a rock covered with velvety moss. She paused to look at the moss and to feel it. As she did, she saw beautiful small pink and blue flowers amidst the smooth moss. She marveled at its beauty. She had not seen anything like it in heaven. She leaned back against the velvety covered rock once again and rested. As she did, she noticed that the tiny flowers released a unique, yet powerful fragrance. Julie closed her eyes and let the fragrance flow over her. She couldn't explain it, but it reminded her of a fragrance that she had known long ago. She continued to rest trying to recall the smell. It was so very intense, yet so pleasant.

Julie smiled to herself as the fragrance began to become vaguely familiar to her.

Ajisth was sitting quietly watching her. "You remember it now, don't you?" he asked softly.

Julie sat up straight. She turned and smiled at Ajisth, and then closed her eyes and took in a deep breath. "I do recognize it," Julie answered Ajisth as she opened her eyes. "But it's sweeter than I ever remember, and much more intense and pure."

"All things are like that here," Ajisth reminded Julie.

"It's absolutely precious," Julie added, with a smile. She then paused and sat up a little straighter, taking in one more deep breath before continuing, "It's the smell of babies," Julie said slowly and remarkably. "It's as if all of heaven just turned into a baby nursery." Julie laughed. "Can there be a smell any more precious?"

Ajisth stood up and reached for Julie's hand. She then took his hand as he pulled her up. They continued to walk upward and Julie knew they were nearing the top.

Ajisth stopped and looked into Julie's eyes to help her to understand. Julie felt the Father's presence surround them and grow more intense. This was one of the great joys of heaven: ever-learning, always a new experience; and more understanding of the many untold mysteries of heaven and earth as they would unfold before you in the most unexpected and beautiful ways.

"This is a beautiful place," Julie exclaimed with excitement as they reached the top.

"The Father wanted you to see this," Ajisth replied smiling.

Julie stood and peered at the valley that lay below her. She could hear the sound of laughter, the laughter of children. It filled the air in a chorus. There was a light mist that hovered over the valley which caused heaven's rays of light to sparkle like diamonds as they shone down upon it. Rainbows darted through the mist. Bright prisms of colors danced all around as if in sync to the musical chorus of the laughter of the children.

Julie studied the valley below and immersed herself in its beauty. "This is just too beautiful to behold," Julie said to Ajisth, smiling more with her heart than her mouth. Her heart overflowed, too full, to take it all in.

"What is this place called?" Julie asked Ajisth.

"Come, walk with me, and I will show you more," Ajisth answered her and smiled.

As they began to walk down into the valley before them, the Father joined them. The sound of the children's laughter was now joined with the voices and sounds of children talking. The sound of their high-pitched little voices filled the air, reminding Julie of the sound of little Smurfs.

As they came out of the mist, Julie stopped suddenly. She paused and glanced at the Father and then at Ajisth. Julie knew that this experience would be a learning experience and not a reunion. But she never expected anything like this.

"This is a very special place, Julie," Father spoke softly.

"A very special place," Julie repeated. She could hardly speak.

"I made it just for them," Father continued. "They love it when the adults come to visit."

Julie stood in awe as she looked out upon the crowd of souls before her. The number was endless, and they filled the whole valley with their presence, as far as Julie could see. Julie remembered the very first baby soul that she had seen in heaven; her dear sweet Michaela. She had seen many other souls of children throughout heaven also, but she had never seen so many of them gathered in one place.

"There are so many of them," Julie remarked, as she turned to the Father and Ajisth. "Who are they?" Julie asked.

"Many would call them the lost souls," Father explained. "But they were never lost. They were always with me and I with them."

"Suffer the little children to come unto me," Ajisth softly quoted the Father's words from so long ago.

"They are so precious," Julie said, her voice filling with strong emotion.

"They have always been precious in my sight," Father said, as he looked out upon them.

Julie gazed into the Father's eyes. She had never seen them filled with such an intense love.

"I knew this would be a very special place for you, Julie," Father explained lovingly as he placed his arm around her. They stood and watched the children play happily.

"These are the children that knew only great sorrow on earth," Father answered Julie's unasked question. "These were the aborted children," her Father continued slowly. "And the older children are the abused ones who died from their abuse. Here, there are no tears. Here, they know only laughter, joy, and love."

"These were the ones whom you cared for so much, Julie," Ajisth added.

"They are so very precious," Julie repeated again and then was speechless to try to say any more.

"We have many reunions here," Ajisth continued.

"Many," the Father repeated.

"Oh!" Julie exclaimed. "It must be wonderful when the mother or father who has been forgiven and redeemed meet their children and their children meet them."

Julie paused and again watched the children laughing and playing. "Are there many that have no parents?"

"Yes," Father answered. "They are content in the love that surrounds them and from all the many souls in heaven who love them. They feel no loss here, only the joy of what they know, and no sorrow for what was or could've been."

Julie noticed a smile cross the Father's face. It glowed with a radiance which Julie had never seen before. She was able to see the Father, Jesus, and his Spirit, all in one. The love for his creation, his children, illuminated heaven brighter than Julie had ever seen it.

Suddenly, the children quieted. And then without warning, they let out a scream of shrill delight and started to run towards them.

"They know that we are here now, Julie," Ajisth announced, and let out a deep laugh.

The Father gave Julie a broad smile. "They will welcome you Julie with much excitement and will want to show you around *'children's gate'*."

The Father and Ajisth began to fade as Julie turned and saw the children running towards her. She did not know any of them but felt an unexplainable love for all of them. She knelt down and reached out to them with open arms. They ran into her arms and she held them tight. She stroked their hair and looked deep into their eyes. She could still feel the Father's strong presence near her and them.

"Can I come here and visit often?" she questioned softly as she gazed up into heaven's light.

"As often, as you like," her Father answered.

"Of course you can come see us," a little girl answered with the Father.

Julie looked down and peered into the little girl's eyes and saw her beautiful soul.

"My name is *Gracie*," the little girl told Julie as she reached for Julie's hand.

Julie wrapped her hand around the little girl's hand tightly.

A little boy took Julie's other hand as more of the children gathered round.

"Come," they called out to Julie, as they tugged at her to follow and walk with them. Julie's heart overflowed as she let them lead her through the valley that was filled with laughter.

"Heaven's Joy"

chapter

15

> "I can safely say,
> on the authority of all that is revealed
> in the Word of God,
> that any man or woman on this earth
> who is bored and turned off by worship
> is not ready for heaven."
> ~ A.W. Tozer

Julie thought there could not be a more precious place in heaven than at *children's gate*. Julie proceeded to walk down the path to go to her favorite place at the waterfall. Those who were dearest to her knew they could often find her there. Michaela visited her there regularly, as did many of her family and other friends. Some of her favorite visits, though, were with Mike. They had shared over a half century of years together as man and wife and had shared their souls in a depth that Julie had shared with no other.

Julie smiled as she sat and watched the water cascade before her. She loved to feel the mist and gentle spray of the water splash upon her with the warmth of heaven's light. Julie marveled at the loss of vision and knowledge from her past life. It was the limitations of her physical mind and body which had impeded and kept her from understanding so much of what the heavenly truly was like. It had troubled her greatly in her earthly mind and thinking to know that there would be no marriage in heaven. She had thought back then, *well, what will become of the love?* But she could never have grasped the understanding of how love does not die nor does it change. The way love is expressed in the finite is only an earnest of the inheritance of love. In heaven, love is expressed in the spiritual. In heaven, love is in its purest form because it is radiating from the source of love, God himself. There are no boundaries on love in heaven. And there is not singular love. Love is love. The love for her one brother differed from her other brothers. Her love for her one friend differed from her other friend. Each soul's love was a special gift in itself; none more, none less; just all unique in their own realm. All the love that we shared with every person, every soul, is expressed in its purest form in heaven. That's why there are such jubilees throughout all of heaven, and joy that overflows at the homecoming of every soul.

"I thought I would find you here." It was Mike's gentle voice as he joined Julie at her favorite spot.

"I love waterfalls," Julie responded as she turned to Mike and smiled. Their eyes met and their souls radiated in the Father's love and presence.

"I know you do," Mike remarked with a slight chuckle. "And the heavenly shores," he added.

"Yes," Julie laughed.

"I can usually find you when you are playing your music," Julie remarked.

"Did you ever picture heaven to be this way?" Mike asked.

"Never," Julie answered. "I still can't imagine all that heaven holds for us," Julie added, and then continued excitedly, "I have a surprise for you."

Mike grinned from ear to ear. "O—kay," he said slowly.

"I've just got to share with you a very special place that the Father and Ajisth took me to earlier."

"A place you had never seen?" Mike asked.

"Yes!" Julie exclaimed.

Mike sat and listened to Julie, hearing the excitement rise in her voice.

"You were always so supportive, Mike, of everything I did in our past."

"I knew your gifts, Julie. It was God's purpose in all that you did."

"I always loved helping the children," Julie continued.

"Even the adults who had lost the child within them," Mike added.

"Yes," Julie nodded and smiled.

"The broken and shattered," Mike continued.

"I've seen a lot of them here," Julie stated happily, "but they are no longer broken and shattered."

"I love the reunions," Mike expressed with his heart as he watched the water ripple downstream. "Especially the unexpected ones."

"Like the one with Michaela?"

"Yes, that was probably one of my most treasured," Mike replied, giving Julie a warm smile. "So what and where is this special place?" he asked.

"Come," Julie answered. She grabbed Mike's hand and pulled him up.

As they walked through heaven's gardens, they stopped and talked to many people along the way. Some of the souls who they met recognized them together because they had remembered them as a couple.

Suddenly, Julie and Mike stopped. And actually, everyone near them also paused. The heavenly light became brighter as they all waited. The sounds of heavenly music became louder with the voices of angels blending in perfect harmony as they rose in praise. All the souls of heaven were lifted up and they too began to lift their hearts in praise. All listened for the sound of the trumpets. All wondered if this could be the day that the trumpet would sound and signal the rapture and call for the many souls on earth to come home.

Julie loved the freedom of heaven—the rapture of love divine. It wasn't that you had to praise God in heaven. It was that your soul loved to be in his presence: a presence of purest love, peace, comfort, and joy. There were no earthly words to describe it for you had to experience it. Julie remembered when the Father's spirit had come into her heart as a child. She thought nothing could surpass that feeling. And then when she was older, she remembered how he had filled her with his presence, engulfing her until her mortal body could receive no more. But even that was just what the Bible called an *earnest* of the inheritance of his spirit. Here in heaven, you received all of it. You would shine as the noon day sun. You rose in jubilation and exultation. Your soul rose on its own in blissful and rapturous adoration to the bosom of your God, Savior, and Father of all creation. Julie had experienced at many times the different revelations of God. She treasured every one of them. But there was just something so magnificent to see God as the mighty Jesus and King. Yes, he was her Father. Yes, he was her Savior. But to behold him as the King of Kings was enrapturing. It empowered and humbled Julie in ways she would never be able to articulate.

They would remain in this moment of praise until the course of heaven turned, engulfed in his presence, indifferent to time, as time did not exist.

And it came to pass, that once and again, Mike and Julie would find themselves walking down the paths of heaven. Julie let God's spirit lead them, for she had no recollection or direction as to how to get to *children's gate* or anywhere in heaven by herself. She walked and somehow just knew the way.

"Let's stop here," Mike suggested.

It was a slightly familiar path for Julie. "Have you been here before, Mike?" she asked.

"No, I don't believe so," Mike answered. "Is it familiar to you?"

"A little," Julie nodded as she glanced around. "The tree over there looks like a cherry tree, and the narrowing path ahead, both seem familiar."

"Well," Mike replied and motioned to Julie, "Why don't we just sit here and see what the Father presents."

Julie smiled. This was one of the great joys of heaven, to watch and let things unfold before you.

At first, Julie wondered if Michaela might join them, or Ajisth, or the Father. As Julie and Mike remained and continued in their deep conversation, they didn't notice that the path before them began to clear until there were no souls walking on it.

Julie had never really been surprised by the appearance of anyone while in heaven. Their presence always seemed to be preceded by a knowledge of it happening. However, this time, Julie and Mike both were a little astonished when they looked up and noticed a man coming towards them. The man paused and watched them before he came closer. Julie had often paused at times like this when approaching someone when she was unsure of what she was to do, especially when there were no others around. There was a sense, at these times that God was doing a work that would unfold with knowledge being revealed.

The man saw Julie and Mike watching him as he slowly walked a little closer towards them. Julie waited and gave the man a kind smile. She recognized him once more as the man who had approached her several times previously. Every time she encountered him, there appeared to be more and more familiarity. Mike waited also, and for some unknown reason, reached and placed his hand over Julie's. Julie could feel their love and strength mount up as the Father's presence increased in their midst.

Mike watched the man. Mike realized this was the man Julie had told him about at various times. However, Mike had never met him. This was his first time, and he was surprised also that he too recognized him but did not have knowledge of him. Julie and Mike both remained silent.

The man took a few more steps closer to them. Julie could see the man's humbled spirit. Again, she couldn't help notice that never in heaven had she seen someone so humbled in their approach to her.

"I hope I am not intruding," he said quietly.

"No," Julie answered with a smile, trying to put the man at ease.

Mike tightened his hand around Julie's and just couldn't figure out in his own heart why the man had such an effect on him. He too noticed the man's humbleness of heart and was puzzled. Mike also had a few encounters such as these with other souls whom he had met; however, never to this degree. He knew that the Father was doing a special work in their midst and waited with Julie.

"May I sit with you?" he asked.

"Yes," both Mike and Julie answered together.

"I was very blinded in times past," he explained in such a low voice that Julie could barely hear him.

"I see now the love that the Father had given to both of you for each other. I wasn't able to see it before I found the Father's love. Now, all things are seen so clearly." The man hesitated before continuing to speak. He glanced at Julie and then at Mike and gave them both a warm and humble smile. Julie was able to see in his eyes the earnestness of wanting to express his sincerity. Mike looked intently at the man and studied him with some confusion. The man then focused his attention on Mike and spoke kindly to him as if to answer his unasked question. "You only knew me in my sinful state, Mike."

Mike nodded to the man and quietly replied, "I understand."

The man then turned his attention once again to Julie and continued, "I was forgiven greatly by you Julie." Julie felt the Father's love radiate through the man.

"And Mike, you supported and encouraged her. I owe a great debt to both of you."

"He paid all of our debts on Calvary," Mike kindly responded.

"We all have sinned and had debts that needed forgiven," Julie added.

"Is this why you don't want the knowledge of who you are revealed?" Julie asked.

"Yes," the man answered.

"But you are forgiven," Mike interjected.

"Yes, I do know this," the man continued. "Until the Father reveals all things, may I tell you both that I have a great love for you and will always appreciate your forgiveness."

"Thank you," Julie answered.

"No need to thank me. Please, I just want to give you both the love, the Father's true love, which you deserved so long ago. It was your love and forgiveness that showed me that the Father's love and forgiveness was possible. I could never believe or understand how God could love or forgive me. I could not love or forgive myself. I could not love or forgive others. I had lost all capacity to love, and yet you forgave me. You forgave me without my even telling you that I was sorry. And I was so very sorry."

This was the first time in heaven that Julie had felt taken aback. She didn't feel sorrow or pain, but rather, she felt a feeling of jubilation. A jubilation that God's love had saved this soul, just as he had saved her soul, and Mike's soul, and every soul that had repented of their sins and turned from their sinful ways.

"It's all about surrender," Julie said to the man.

The man smiled a warm smile. "That is what you used to always tell me."

Julie couldn't remember the kind smile.

"It's because I don't believe I ever gave you a warm or kind smile," the man said, as if reading Julie's mind.

Mike let the man and Julie talk. He felt, by the guiding of his spirit, that he was just to be there with the Father's presence as they spoke.

"You had told me I had to confess all of my sins if I was to be saved. And I didn't want to believe that I had any sins. I always tried to convince you I did nothing wrong even though I knew in my heart that I had broken and shattered you."

Julie could not respond. She had never had an experience like this before.

"You told me that I must quit minimizing, justifying, and denying my sins; and make it right with God."

"I was pretty bold," Julie softly acknowledged.

"Oh, but you had to be," the man answered back swiftly, yet kindly, as if he had to share this with her.

Julie felt the Father's presence grow strongly upon her. She felt his love flow over her and fortify her as she looked deeply into the man's eyes and saw his redeemed soul. Julie then felt led to reach out and to take his hand into hers.

The man could feel the Father's love flow through Julie to him.

"We must let the Father unfold all things," Julie expressed softly and gently. "We will all understand the great mysteries of heaven by and by."

"By and by," the man repeated her words with a sincere smile.

Julie studied the man's kind smile. It touched her heart in a special way. She turned to Mike, whose eyes were upon her, and then she turned back to the man. However, he had departed.

Mike and Julie said nothing to one another as they felt the peace of heaven and the Father's love flow over them. Heaven's light emanated down upon them and there was no need for words. They both had an inner peace, and knew that things would unfold in the Father's way and they would understand all things more fully then.

After a while, Mike turned to Julie and asked, "Can we go to see your surprise?"

"Yes!" Julie answered with excitement.

They walked down the narrow path together and talked, allowing the Spirit to lead them as they had done all of their lives before. Shortly, they were at the mountain top.

Mike looked down into the valley and heard the musical chorus of children's laughter rising up to meet them. Angels joined in the chorus and filled the air. The Father's presence glistened through heaven's light and once again settled down upon them.

"What is this place?" Mike asked smiling.

"Come on," Julie exclaimed excitedly, as she tugged at Mike's hand. "I'll show you. It's called, *children's gate.*"

Together, hand in hand, they walked down the path and into the children's waiting arms.

God's Revealing Light

chapter

16

"Faith is the strength by which a shattered world
shall emerge into the light."
~ Helen Keller

Of all the things that Julie had learned in heaven, one of the most profound was how meticulously and spectacularly God had orchestrated every specific thing in heaven. From the beginning of creation to the present era, God always had a plan. It was all in his Word, laid out as a blueprint, verse by verse, prophecy by prophecy, fulfillment upon fulfillment, for every dispensation.

The beauty of it all was that every soul, every soul, had a purpose—from those who felt they were the lowliest, to those who had led as patriarchs and matriarchs for their God. Those who had been blind, handicapped, or mentally incapacitated were received into heaven with the same honor and bore as many stars in their crowns as any other soul. Just as the beggar man Lazarus, who had been treated as useless, of no value, or purpose, in that world; in heaven, he was revered, and honored by all the host of heaven.

Every soul had a purpose—an important purpose. Everything they had, or had not done, either led them to or distracted them from that purpose. There was not a thing given to any soul without it fulfilling a God-given purpose. Those who felt as though they were without any gifts and felt surely they could not have accomplished anything for the kingdom of heaven were shocked to find out that every act, even the simplest of acts they had done by faith for God's kingdom, had impacted souls.

That was the other thing that just mesmerized Julie. Every soul from the beginning of creation, even to the current dispensation, impacted other souls. No soul ever lived, or was created in the womb, who did not impact other lives, both in their present life and for generations to come.

Julie had grown in knowledge as the Father had unveiled many of the mysteries of heaven. He had revealed to all of them that this connection is what made them truly all one. Every life, every soul, every one of God's creation, and every child impacted other's lives. Every soul mattered. Every soul had a purpose. Every soul made a difference and had a part in the plan of God for their lives, and also for every soul they met.

Julie had experienced many things in heaven. The jubilees and reunions were still some of her favorites. The stories of the reunions, and of the redeemed, caused every soul to rejoice.

Julie had heard many stories of the redeemed. The story of how just one smile from a young woman to an elderly lady had given the elderly woman hope to live. She had already planned to take her life that day, but that simple act of love had changed everything. Later the woman was redeemed.

There was story after story of such encounters—the soldier who died on the battlefield for another; the little boy who dove into the water to save a friend and then perished himself; the rescue worker who saved a baby in the fire and then later succumbed from his burns; the child who died from a rare disease; the family killed by a drunk driver; the child who had been abused; the woman who had been raped; the man who had been murdered. All of the tragic, merciless deeds, diseases, and defects were all explained in heaven.

Here, one saw how God was never the cause of these tragedies but rather the solution. It was mankind that had made the choices that perpetuated the evil that had fallen upon man. From the first choice given to Adam and Eve, throughout every generation, down through all the ages, man's choices had filtered down to create the fallen world and brought it to the state that it was in. God had never desired for mankind to suffer, for children to die of disease, for souls to be murdered, injured, or maimed. His desire for mankind had been the Garden of Eden. But even then, God had planned to die for his children. The plan of Calvary was carved in God's plan before creation itself.

All of the questions Julie had ever asked, and so many more, were answered in heaven. All that could not be understood in the past was given complete clarity in heaven. The amazing thing was that one could see how God had taken all the tragedies of life, and all the lives that had been impacted, and had woven them into an intricacy of love, hope, and promise. Some of this would not be seen or fulfilled for generations to come.

Many rejected God because of the tragedies, blaming him as the cause, the great omnipotent God, whom they felt had looked the other way. They had felt that God's ear was heavy and could not hear and that his arm was short and could not save.

Mankind had forgotten, and even refused to see, the evil forces and stronghold that Lucifer himself had imposed on mankind, and upon the free gift of choice that God had given man. Mankind had long lost sight of the spiritual warfare raging in the heavenlies and on earth. They forgot that we wrestle not against flesh and blood, but against principalities, against powers, against the rulers of the darkness of this world, against spiritual wickedness in high places. They had long forgotten that God loved them, confused by their own lack of understanding, hurt and pain. They chose to turn to their own thoughts, their own understanding, and to find their own way. They deviated from all that God's word declared and created their own standards of what was right and what was wrong. They refused to surrender to a God they could not trust and did not believe in. They created their own beliefs, based upon their own desires, wants, and pride of life. Often, they would weave a little of God into these beliefs to assuage their guilt. They called this religion and let it replace God's original plan of relationship. They found themselves lost, angry, and bitter.

And soon, very soon, all would change in a twinkling of an eye. All of heaven waited for the time to come when the great trumpet would sound. All of heaven prepared for that time with great expectation. First would come the Rapture, and then the seven years of Tribulation, followed by Armageddon, a thousand years of peace, Satan loosed for a short time and then banished forever, the Great White Throne Judgment, and then the New Heaven and New Earth, and the New Jerusalem.

All of this had seemed so impossible in her humanity; however, heaven had taught Julie many things. So many of the mysteries of heaven she now understood. Every day, there were new revelations of the mysteries of old. It didn't seem difficult for Julie to comprehend all that was before them and yet to come.

Oh the joy and splendor of heaven, Julie thought. She wondered, *Could she ever grasp the reality of it all?* But yes, heaven was more real than her earthly life had ever been. She marveled at the love that had drawn her to salvation and it humbled her. *How could I, of all the souls, been blessed to know the Savior?*

"It was *Amazing Grace*," Ajisth spoke up softly as he joined Julie.

Julie turned and smiled at Ajisth. "You are right, Ajisth. It was his *Amazing Grace*." Julie looked up at the heavenly light shining down upon them. "I could have never fathomed heaven."

"Most cannot, Julie," Ajisth replied, beckoning Julie to come.

"Are we going somewhere?" Julie asked with a smile on her face.

"Yes," Ajisth answered, giving Julie a mischievous smile.

"Where?" Julie asked curiously.

"Come," is all Ajisth would say.

"You know," Julie said half kidding, "sometimes you don't have much to say."

Ajisth only smiled and nodded at Julie.

Julie paused and then asked, "Well?"

"Well, what?" Ajisth answered.

"Are you going to tell me where we're going?" Julie asked softly.

Ajisth took Julie's hand and gently led her forward. "The Father wanted me to bring you to him."

"But this is not the way that we usually go to the garden," Julie remarked.

Again, Ajisth smiled and said, "I know. It's a special place, Julie."

"So are we not going to the garden?" Julie asked.

"No," Ajisth replied.

"Oh," Julie responded as she began to feel the Father's presence surround them. His presence grew stronger and stronger as they neared the place where the Father awaited her.

A Small Gate in
the Distance

chapter

17

"We are made wise not by the recollection of our past,
but by the responsibility of our future."
~ George Bernard Shaw

There was a small gate in the distance. Julie had never seen it before. It was a beautiful simple gate covered by an arbor. As Julie and Ajisth drew nearer, Julie noticed that it was covered in flowers. The flowers, with their sweet fragrance, filled the air and tickled Julie's nose.

Julie began to feel the music as they entered through the gate. The sound of the angels singing ushered her into the full presence of the Father.

They walked down what appeared to be a small trail where the path had narrowed. Julie could see a stream in the distance. As they drew nearer, she could hear the water rustle loudly through the mountainside as the gurgling sounds of the rapids tumbled over the rocks. A carpet of soft moss covered the ground upon the path that they walked. Julie felt its softness under her feet. Wild flowers grew throughout the free-flowing garden. Trees hung over the path, creating an archway above them. The trees were covered with flowers that Julie had never seen before. The flowers were of so many different colors, glimmering and sparkling in heaven's light.

"What a beautiful, quaint garden," Julie remarked, smiling as she took in the beauty surrounding her.

Up ahead, Julie noticed an older woman sitting on a bench. She appeared to be enjoying watching the stream as it rushed past her. Her back was turned opposite of Julie concealing her identity. Julie wasn't able to see who it was.

"I thought you said we were going to see the Father?" Julie asked Ajisth.

"I did," Ajisth answered softly.

"But?" Julie began to speak.

"Come," Ajisth said tenderly. He patted Julie's hand as he held it.

There was no fear, just anticipation. Julie and Ajisth walked on and approached the elderly woman. Julie began to feel a familiarity as the woman turned slowly and faced Julie. She smiled happily and jumped up. "Well, Julie, I didn't know that I would get to see you so soon."

"I had no idea either, Gramma," Julie exclaimed, giving her gramma a big hug.

Julie gazed into her gramma's eyes. She remembered those beautiful eyes. They were soft and narrow. It was a family trait that showed up very dominantly throughout all of their family.

Julie slid her arm through her gramma's arm, linking them together, and they continued to walk down the winding path.

"Isn't it beautiful here, Gramma?" Julie asked.

"Oh, I love it here," she replied.

"Do you come here often?" Julie continued to ask.

"Quite often," Gramma replied with a big smile.

Ajisth walked beside Julie on her other side and drew nearer to her as they rounded the bend in the path.

There, standing quietly, was the man who Julie had encountered so many times on her walks. She watched as he walked slowly towards them.

"Do you know him, Gramma?" Julie asked.

Her gramma did not answer but turned and tenderly smiled at Julie. She patted Julie's hand and held it affectionately at her side.

As the man approached them, they all stopped to wait. Julie looked past the man and saw what appeared to be a tiny cottage with a small porch. God's heavenly light began to shine down brighter upon her as she felt the Father's presence increase.

The man smiled at Julie's gramma as he met them. He then reached for her gramma's other hand and took it gently into his. Julie could feel a strong connection between the three of them as she continued to hold her gramma's hand.

The man looked at Julie's gramma and then searched Julie's face. Julie peered into the man's eyes and for the first time recognized the family resemblance. Ajisth remained beside Julie's side and quietly watched.

"You were family?" Julie responded slowly as she began to realize the connection.

"Yes …," the man answered softly.

As they stood in the quietness of the moment, Julie was not able to gain any more knowledge of who the man was.

Ajisth then gently took Julie's arm and began to lead her to the cottage. The man joined them as they began to walk down the path. Julie turned to beckon her gramma to come with them, but saw her standing off to the side. She smiled and lovingly called out to Julie, "I will see you later," and then she faded into the distance.

A Revealing Encounter...

chapter
18

"Never does the human soul appear
so strong and noble
as when it forgoes revenge
and dares to forgive an injury."
~ Edwin Hubbell Chapin

Julie could hear the angels singing ever so softly in the midst. As she approached the cottage, their song began to change, crescendoing and rising into a sweet harmonic melody that filled the air. Julie could feel the Father's presence increase as they neared the cottage. The flowers began to release a sweet smell as if for this occasion. Julie walked closely beside Ajisth as he led them to the porch of the cottage.

Julie wasn't surprised to see the Father sitting there, waiting for her. She broke away and ran to greet him. Ajisth and the man soon followed and joined Julie on the porch. Ajisth sat down next to Julie who was now sitting by the Father's side. The man sat down on a small wooden bench across from them.

Julie couldn't help wonder what all of this meant, but she felt peaceful in the Father's presence.

Julie searched the man's face. He looked deeply into Julie's eyes and smiled. Julie again recognized the familiarity as she studied his eyes and saw the family resemblance, but the one thing she could not recall was his smile.

"You are family?" Julie asked, rather than stated.

"Yes," the man softly replied.

Julie felt the Father's presence overshadow her and his love surround her. Julie felt a strength within her very soul that she couldn't recall ever feeling in heaven.

There was a brief silence as Julie continued to look at the man as he looked at her. The Father's presence had now completely enveloped her.

Julie suddenly began to feel a knowledge of who this mysterious stranger really was. The Father slowly started to open her eyes and began to reveal him to her.

Julie remained quiet as the familiarity started to become a little clearer. It was as if watching a cloud fade slowly into a fine mist, and then disappear, as the revelation unfolded.

Julie closed her eyes. In her thoughts she could envision the family playing horseshoes. She could see her brothers running over the hillside with her, laughing, with their little dog Mamie chasing after them. Julie saw herself and her brothers swimming in the river, skipping rocks, and hiking through the mountains. She saw them taking care of each other, nursing each other when they were hurt, encouraging each other when they were sad. Intermittently, she would see her mom in the pictures that played before her. Julie smiled with love as she saw her mom hugging them. But then, intertwined throughout the memories, she saw him, the man who now sat with them—this mysterious man, whom throughout all of heaven, she had not been able to recognize or gain knowledge of who he was. He appeared so different now. Julie understood then why she had not been able to recognize him. It was as if he was two different people.

Julie slowly opened her eyes. She looked at the soul before her, who was now holding the Father's other hand. Julie gripped the Father's hand tightly as she continued to feel his loving and secure grip upon hers.

Julie looked intensely into the man's eyes and he looked intently into hers. With all that Julie didn't know, she knew this person had impacted her life greatly and that she had impacted his life also. As she peered into his soul, in this wonderful place where thoughts transcend words, and where words are felt more than expressed, she felt a peace that passed all understanding. Here, in this spiritual realm, where life is not confined by the finite, or by the physical, but where life itself lives free from the bondage of fear and shame, guilt and blame, and sin, she began to understand. Here in this unexplainable place, where redemption is lived, not merely given, her eyes were opened.

"You led me to the Father," the man broke his silence.

Julie continued to look deeply into his eyes, reading his spirit, before the words were spoken. The Father lovingly watched as his presence covered them.

"How?" Julie asked a little puzzled as she continued to look into the man's eyes.

There was such a revelation of emotion now radiating from this man of joy, gladness, thankfulness, and love. He looked at the Father. Julie followed his gaze. She watched as the Father nodded slowly for him to continue.

Julie again looked into his eyes as he looked humbly into hers. "How did I impact your life?" Julie now asked more directly.

The man paused once more. The Father's presence flowed over him to where Julie could see into his very soul. Julie saw the humbleness in his spirit. She was even able to see the healed brokenness which had surrounded his heart at one time.

"My brokenness had made me mean, bitter, hard, and cruel," he began. "I had no excuses. I laid them down on that last day when you spoke to me, the day you forgave me."

Julie glanced at the Father and then back at the man. She slowly continued to understand, as the Father unveiled how the man had appeared those many years ago. Julie watched the familiar form evolve before her.

At first, he was a little boy, one who she had remembered seeing long ago in an old faded picture, and then as a teenager on his bike that he rode to work at the Western Union. Julie remembered seeing a photo of him on that same bike. And then she saw him rapidly transform before her. It was as if a movie was playing quickly before her, displaying the man whom she had known throughout her childhood.

Julie blinked her eyes and rubbed them as the familiarity of the soul in front of her conflicted with the images that she now recalled in knowledge. Though she had no recollection of sorrow and pain, she could feel and sense that the soul who stood before her was different than the soul that had impacted her life. This soul was redeemed. He was free of the shackles, torments, and pain that had etched his face in her memories. She had only known him unredeemed until that last day before he had died when she had visited him in the hospital and talked to him.

Julie paused. She looked, once again, gazing intently into the man's eyes, and then spoke. "I told you that day that I forgave you. And you said … ."

"You will never know what that meant to me," the man finished her sentence.

Julie nodded to him and continued to look into his eyes as his familiarity continued to become a little clearer.

She recalled from her past the final look he had given her. He now had that same look in his eyes as he sat before her. It was the look of *redemption*.

"You forgave me, and then I knew," the man continued. "I knew that I could be forgiven. I knew that God could forgive me."

"I understand now," Julie interjected the words intermittently.

"Do you, Julie?" the man asked.

"Yes," Julie answered. This was a new experience for Julie. She could not speak. She did not want to speak. She only wanted to have the Father unveil the knowledge completely.

The man waited in the silence. He also awaited the Father's presence to reveal the unknown.

The knowledge Julie had received from the Father opened her eyes in a way she had never experienced in heaven. There was no sorrow, or pain, as God had taken all of that from her; first in the earthly, when she had forgiven the man, and now also, in this heavenly place. God's presence completely covered Julie as he revealed to her the truth, a truth causing Julie to realize the magnitude of the situation, and the understanding of the apprehension that the man had shown. She now realized this man was her earthly dad.

"I treated you horribly," her dad quietly declared. "I abused you, Julie."

"I know," Julie replied, as she searched the man's eyes. "I see now," Julie continued, her eyes speaking more into the man's soul than her words that followed. "But you are forgiven."

"Yes, I know," the man humbly replied.

"So you did make it right with God, Dad, before you died?"

"I did, Julie," the man answered repentantly. "Do you remember that last day in the hospital when you visited me?"

Julie let the Father reveal it to her spirit. "Yes," Julie answered. "I told you that if you never made it right with me to make it right with God."

"Do you remember what else you told me?" he asked.

Julie then smiled at the man and replied, "I told you quite a lot that day. I was pretty direct with you."

"But there were several things you really pressed onto my heart, my cold and hardened heart that was refusing every word you said to me."

Julie nodded and thought it would help him if she just allowed him to talk.

"Strange," the man continued. "Down there, I thought I had an answer for everything. I could outtalk everyone then. Well, I thought I could. But not you Julie. You were relentless that day."

"I was," Julie agreed emphatically and unabated.

"But amidst all of our conversation that day, one of the first things you told me was, 'I forgive you, Dad.'"

"Yes."

"You forgave me and I didn't deserve it. I couldn't even tell you I was sorry. And still, you forgave me. You read it to me from the Bible, and you wouldn't back down."

"You told me that you did pray," Julie added. "You asked me very roughly, how could I know that you had not made it right with God?"

"And you came right back at me," the man replied.

"Yes," Julie agreed and then continued, "And you being ignorant of God's righteousness went about to establish your own righteousness, having not submitted yourself unto the righteousness of God."

"Yes," her dad replied, "You read that right from your Bible. And then you flipped the pages right to another place without hesitating and read, 'If we say that we have fellowship with him and walk in darkness, we lie, and do not tell the truth. If we say that we have no sin, we deceive ourselves, and the truth is not in us. If we say that we have not sinned, we make him a liar, and his word is not in us. If we confess our sins, he is faithful and just to forgive us our sins, and to cleanse us from all unrighteousness.'"

"Talking to you that day was probably one of the most difficult things I had ever done in my whole lifetime," Julie remarked, expressing every word very candidly with this man who was her earthly dad.

He paused and then peered into Julie's eyes and smiled a gentle smile of kindness. Julie felt a perfect peace and love in the Father's presence. However, the man's smile still puzzled her.

"It puzzles you because I never gave you a smile of kindness or love," the man said, seeing Julie's puzzled expression. "I wasn't redeemed. You only saw the sinful dad. That's why you couldn't recognize me here."

"Yes, I do realize that now. You look nothing like the man I knew then," Julie added.

"I would have died lost," the man earnestly admitted. "All these things you told me that day … you pleaded with me to make it right with God. No matter how much I hammered back at you, you would not let go."

Julie smiled again, seeing the soul who sat before her. "God had told me before I visited you that I was to do two things that day. One, that you must ask God to forgive you; and second, that I was to face my *giant* and"… Julie paused, "and … ."

"You are my giant," the man finished the words Julie had spoken to him that day.

"You were my giant, Dad," Julie repeated.

"But then you prayed for me."

"You let me pray for you," Julie interjected. "You had never let me pray for you. Even when you had your stroke eight years earlier, you had told me, 'Don't come if you are going to talk about Jesus.'"

"And you didn't come," her dad continued.

"I told you that I never leave home without him," Julie replied firmer than she had ever spoken to anyone in heaven.

"You would never let go of my soul. But why?" the man asked.

The Father let the two of them continue to talk. He had planned this time for this very purpose. Ajisth sat quietly also and listened to them.

Julie felt the Father's presence completely cover her. She could feel his presence radiate through her. She once again looked into the man's eyes, into his very soul, so that he would feel the Father's love through her and then answered his question. "Because God never let go of your soul. He told me to come to you. He told me he would not lead me to you if your heart intended evil for me. He protected and covered me with his presence."

"He redeemed me, Julie. I gave my heart to him and asked for his forgiveness as you prayed for me that day. Something changed at that very moment. I wanted to tell you then, but I couldn't say the words."

Julie studied the man before her. For the first time, she could truly see his soul. He transformed once again before her, from the young man on his bicycle, to the young man in his Marine uniform, to the dad she knew and feared terribly as a little girl, to the man he was right before he died. "I knew something had happened," Julie recounted.

"How?" he asked.

"Because when I turned to leave your room, I looked back several times."

"I remember you did. Why?" her dad asked.

"Because every time I looked at you, it was gone."

"What was gone?" he asked softly.

"The look in your eyes," Julie answered. "I kept looking back, thinking I'd catch the look in your eyes, but it was gone."

"What look?" he asked again, inquisitively.

"You always had a look of contempt, anger, arrogance, and control. And they were all gone. Instead, I saw a remorse in your eyes. I had never seen remorse in your eyes, not ever."

"I remember that, Julie. As you walked away, and looked back that last time, I truly realized then what I had lost, and what I had shattered."

Julie continued to stare at the man before her. The completion of this reunion could never be explained in words. It could only be felt in the Father's presence. There was a preciousness in the moment, a time of complete restoration. Julie and her dad both looked at the Father. His love overflowed upon them in gentle waves, immersing them in his presence, and illuminating through them until all of heaven radiated from God's light.

Heaven's Light

chapter
19

Julie continued to enjoy all the beauty of heaven. Every day, there were new mysteries unveiled. Every day, there were more celebrations, reunions, and jubilees. She learned more and more of what would soon come to pass, and earnestly awaited, with all of heaven, the sounding of the trumpet that would usher in the fulfillment of things to come.

Oh, how she wished, she could go back for just a moment and let others know the true reality of this place called heaven: where love has no beginning, and it has no end; where the mercy of God transcends each soul with his divine love and offers us the unmerited forgiveness of our sins.

Julie recalled an old song they used to sing so long ago when she was just a child at the little country church where she had attended. She began to sing it as she walked through heaven's gate and into the gardens. *"Mercy there was great, and grace was free, pardon there was multiplied to me. There my burdened soul found liberty, at Calvary." Divine mercy,* Julie thought. *Mercy that can never be understood in the finite mind, only experienced in the heart and soul.*

Ajisth joined her as he so often did. Heaven's light gleamed down in bright beautiful rays, radiating the Father's omnipresence, ever with her. "Where shall we go today?" she asked Ajisth.

"Julie," Ajisth answered smiling, "There is no today here."

"I know," Julie responded with a chuckle. "Will I ever see all of heaven?" Julie asked.

"No," Ajisth answered. "It is too vast."

"I go to prepare a place for you," Julie quoted from the book of John.

"If it were not true, I would have told you so," Ajisth quoted the rest.

"In my Father's house are many mansions," Julie added. "So many mansions."

"All of what the Father promised, and more," Ajisth continued.

Julie wondered if she would ever understand all the beauty and mysteries of heaven. "People don't understand the reality of heaven, Ajisth."

"It is grace," Ajisth explained. "They don't understand grace."

"It is amazing grace," Julie reiterated.

"The simple personification of what amazing grace truly is— the unmerited favor and unconditional love of God—so simple, so true, so divine." Ajisth replied.

"I thought I understood what grace truly was," Julie continued, "but I didn't know how powerful grace truly is."

"*Amazing Grace, how sweet the sound,*" Ajisth echoed the words of the old hymn.

"*That saved a wretch like me. I once was lost but now I'm found. Was blind but now I see,*" Julie joined in with Ajisth, singing the words.

"And your favorite?" Ajisth asked, knowing the answer.

"*When we've been there ten thousand years. Bright shining as the sun. We've no less days to sing God's praise than when we first begun.*"

"Amazing Grace," Ajisth echoed softly.

"Has it been ten thousand years yet, Ajisth?" Julie asked.

"I have no idea," Ajisth answered. "Does it matter, Julie?"

"No," Julie answered. "No, it does not matter at all." Julie beheld the heavenly light that continually radiated down upon her and all of heaven. The walls and foundations were garnished with many precious stones of jasper, sapphire, chalcedony, emerald, sardonyx, sardius, chrysolite, beryl, topaz, chrysoprasus, jacinth, and amethyst. These were colors of deep red, dark blue, white, light blue, brilliant green, shining black onyx, shimmering lime green, and crystals of all colors: orange, yellow, and purple, all the colors of the rainbow, all translucent and iridescent, all sparkling in heaven's light. All twelve of the gates were pearl; the streets of gold glistened and were clear as glass.

"There is nothing like it," Ajisth said, giving Julie a smile. "None of creation has been created more beautiful or specifically designed than heaven for God's children."

"And," Julie added, "the Bible says, 'The heaven of heavens cannot contain him.'"

"Eye has not seen, nor ear heard, neither has entered into the heart of man, the things which God has prepared for them that love him," Mike added with a big smile.

"Mike, where did you come from?" Julie asked surprised and happy to see him.

"Oh, from over at the east gate," he answered.

They walked on, and on, through the many gardens, others joining them along the way. They walked past the river of the water of life, and past the clear and crystal sea, flowing from the throne of God and of the Lamb, and then joined with the throng of angels at the rejoicing of another jubilee. Music filled the air and encompassed their very being. Worship lifted them high into God's presence as sweet aromas of praise and fragrances filled their senses. Here they entered into a rest that was eternal, into a love that did not end, and into the holy presence, of *"Heaven's Light!"*

Amazing Grace

Epilogue

Amazing Grace: Heaven's Light is more than just another story about heaven. It is a story about love, hope, joy, and peace, and a story about closure. *Amazing Grace* is a story of the reality of a God, a Savior, a Jesus, who truly does love us; it's a story of a God to whom we not only matter, but a God who desires to take us under His wing, hide us in the cleft of the rock, and comfort us for an eternity.

My desire in writing *Amazing Grace* was that the reader may come to know this "Amazing Grace" and may be drawn to "Heaven's Light." Within these pages, my prayer was that one would know and see the deep reality of God and the surety of a heaven that awaits. "I go to prepare a place for you," Jesus declared, "Here there are many mansions. If it were not true, I would have told you so."

There is a purpose to our being, a purpose to our life. Yes, "life is a vapor that appears for a little while and then vanishes away." But we are so much more than a vapor. Can we see that our life, each individual life, is a creation of divine purpose? Whether great or small in man's summation, to God, we are highly favored in His eyes because we are His children, His very own. Truly without doubt, heaven is for real, and this life is to prepare us for that wonderful place called home. Heaven is not God's afterthought of a life well-lived here below, but rather, it's a beacon of light leading us, even beckoning us, to know that in heaven, herein lies the reality of all that we ever desired and hoped for. How shallow and empty this life will seem when we step into those portals of infinite love and grace.

There are many themes running through this story of *Amazing Grace: Heaven's Light.* I hope that you have been drawn into the "more" that awaits us. Yes, the beauty of heaven, the omnipresent and omnipotent love of a Father and Savior who has never been a God that is far off, but always an ever-present presence within our hearts and lives. He is a God who has always walked beside us and desired to live in us, waiting on us to simply ask Him to come into our hearts.

Amazing Grace is a wonderful story of the miracle and revelation of, yes, beautiful reunions and wonderful jubilees. But it is more. It is a story of the divine importance of our very salvation, of the redeemed and the unredeemed, of a heaven to gain and a hell to shun, of angels and purpose, of an eternity that is truly the beginning and not the end. It may leave you with many unanswered questions and with much soul searching. It may leave you with an understanding that God and heaven are no more mystical, as a dream untold, but a divine presence and place that has been long awaiting our appearing. "We are expected."

A strong thread and theme throughout *Amazing Grace* is the true experience of forgiveness—our forgiveness and our forgiveness of others. Never could we realize the impact of the power that forgiveness has on our soul and the souls of others. In forgiveness we are set free. Forgiveness is the ultimate surrender to a God who knows all; a God who not only will take our frailty, our failures, our mistakes, and yes, our sins, and through it all will cleanse us and redeem us. He who said, "If my people who are called by my name will humble themselves, and pray, and seek my face, and turn from their wicked ways, then will I hear from heaven, and hear their cry and forgive their sins … ." He who said, "Come unto me, you who are weary and heavy laden, and I will give you rest." And He who says, "If we will confess our sins, He is faithful and just to forgive us our sins. But if we say that we have no sin, then we make Him a liar and His truth is not in us." If we truly lean on our supposed good works, then we nullify His love for us, make salvation our own works, and make his death in vain. For truly there is a heaven to gain, and a hell to shun. To deny either is to make eternity once again a mystical place, where its reality fades from our hearts and minds.

Amazing Grace beckons you to step into God's grace, come up higher, and experience the reality of your Father's love. Many asked Peter those many years ago, shortly after Jesus had ascended into heaven, "What must we do to be saved?" Wherein, Peter answered their question so unequivocally, so non-religiously of tenet or doctrine, and simply replied "Repent, and be baptized in the name of Jesus, for the remission of your sins, and you shall be filled with the Holy Spirit. For this promise is to you, and to your children, and to your children's children, even as many as the Lord our God shall call." Salvation is not a religious oracle to fear, but it is a gift of eternity given to us by the One who loves us, died for us, and gave His life for us, that we may not only know but experience this great joy of redemption.

My heart's desire is that in reading *Amazing Grace: Heaven's Light* you will be drawn into His everlasting love for you and that you may experience the light of His presence and reality. Truly you are fearfully made, and as Isaiah once said, "You are never forgotten and are carved in the palm of His hand." How precious you are to Him, more costly than gold, with an infinite purpose. You are a child of God, created in His image, destined for a place that is home. A home that is filled with "Amazing Grace and Heaven's Light."

God's richest blessings.
~Marsha (Marty) Barth

About the Author

Marsha Lynn Barth (Marty) is an author and inspirational speaker. She has spoken at various retreats and conferences for 20 years. She has done many radio interviews across the nation as far away as Hawaii, and in other countries, and interviewed on TV to bring a message of healing to the broken and shattered. As a speaker she has spoken to college Criminology and Psychology students; for the University of Hawaii; to State Social Services programs involving advocates and foster parents; to addiction and recovery centers; and at child advocacy venues. She has talked personally to her current Pennsylvania State Governor and has been a guest speaker for PCAR (Pennsylvania Coalition Against Rape) at their state event, speaking with State Representatives, the former Governor's wife, and other state leaders, to bring awareness, prevention, and the importance of knowing the joy of overcoming—going from "Victim to Victor." Marsha has DJ'd on Christian radio and worked at a drug rehab hospital. But dearest to her heart, she has visited and spoken at prisons in Pennsylvania for over 15 years and has been a guest speaker in prisons across the nation and as far away as Maui and Kauai, Hawaii, Florida, Virginia, and at an all-male facility maximum-security prison in Maryland.

Marsha was born in the foothills of West Virginia. A business-woman by profession, she ran the family business side by side with her husband Mike in Pennsylvania for nearly 27 years. She is the mother of two children, Mike Jr. and Jennifer, and has ten grand-children—nine boys and one girl.

Marty, as she prefers to be called, is an author, speaker, and advocate. Her book *The Shattering: A Child's Innocence Betrayed* is her true life story of overcoming child sexual abuse. More than a story of victimization, it is a story of the power of love, the promise of hope, and the joy of overcoming. *The Shattering II: Breaking the Silence* was endorsed by Congresswoman Mauree Gingrich and takes the reader on a healing journey, past the pain, from *"Victim to Victor."* Written in novel form, both books reveal to the reader how just one thread of hope can truly change a life. *Tony, The Lonely Dandelion*, endorsed by Shannon Peduto, Executive Director of Luzerne County Child Advocacy Center, is a children's book on bullying. *Amazing Grace: Heaven's Light* is an inspiring novel, full of mystery and intrigue, written so that your eyes may get a glimpse of the reality of heaven and the reality of a God who loves you more than you could have ever imagined.

It is Marty's goal to let the broken and shattered know that they do matter, and that they may know the reality of a God who truly does love and care for them, and their every heartfelt hopes and dreams. That we all may know we can heal, and understand that healing is a journey that will lead us to God's heart and purpose for our lives—"our happiness and our salvation."

Marty is an avid teacher, speaker, and advocate, and is avail-able for speaking events. She draws from her life's experiences and brings forth a message of hope to the broken, hopeless, abused, and shattered.

Contact Marsha Barth for speaking and teaching engagements, for her studies on "Victim to Victor, The Healing Journey, The Pathway to Healing and for more studies and information, please contact her at:

E-mail: mbarthmbarth@gmail.com

Web Page: https://marshabarth.com

Facebook: https://www.facebook.com/
The-Shattering-215752548593960

Linked In: https://www.linkedin.com/in/
marsha-marty-barth-9865a840/

Twitter: https://twitter.com/mbarthmbarth

You Tube: https://www.youtube.com/channel/
UCdegaQc92g8vLHeB7KDJaUw

Many may wonder after reading *Amazing Grace: Heaven's Light* what was the subject of the injustice that was done to Julie that she had to find the grace, strength, and path to forgive the mysterious stranger that continually met her throughout this book. You will find more of this story in the following books written by Marsha Barth.

The Shattering: A Child's Innocence Betrayed
The Shattering II: Breaking the Silence

Tony the Lonely Dandelion

Never "The End"...

Only
"The Beginning"

Scripture References
Referred to in this Book

Revelation Chapter 21—**Heaven's light, description of heaven**

Matthew 7:13-14; Proverbs 14:12; Isaiah 30:21—**Choices**

2 Corinthians 5:1-9—**Mortal and earth-to heavenly**

Revelations 1:8,11; Revelations 21:6; 22:13—**Alpha and Omega**

Revelations 22—**Heaven, river of life, heaven's light, tree of life**

Matthew 7:13-14—**The strait path**

Philippians 3:21—**glorious body**

Matthew 24:31—**Angels, sound of the trumpet, gathering together**

Revelation 21:23—**Heaven's Light**

John 14:2-3—**Many mansions**

Peter 3:8—**A day as a year-a year as a day**

2 Corinthians 5:8—**Absent from the body ... present with the Lord**

1 Corinthians 2:9—**Eye has not seen, ear heard—what God has prepared ...**

Matthew 22:30—**No marriage in heaven ... are as the angels of God ...**

Luke 16:19-31—**The rich man and Lazarus—memories**

1 Corinthians 13:12— ... **But then shall I know even as also I am known ...**

Philippians 4:7—**Peace that passes understanding ...**

Jeremiah 1:5—**Before you were in the womb, I knew you ...**

Mark 14:25—**Fruit of the vine until I drink it new in the kingdom of God**

Revelation 4:6 and 15:2—**Sea of Glass**

Revelation 5:8—**Golden vials full of odours (fragrant)-prayers of saint**

Psalm 150—**Praise in heaven-trumpets, harp, timbrel, stringed, organ**

Revelation 14:2-3—**Harps, sung a new song**

Luke 15:7—**Joy in heaven over one sinner who repents**

Revelation 5:11—**I heard the voice of many angels—10,000 x 10,000**

Revelation 5:12—**Saying with a loud voice—Worthy is the Lamb slain ...**

Ezekiel 28—**The fate of Lucifer-the fallen angel**

Isaiah 14:12—**The fall of Lucifer**

Exodus 30:7-8; 2 Chronicles 13:11—**Every morning and evening incense**

Matthew 18:10—**Children's guardian angels.**

Revelation 21:4—**No sorrow, no pain, no tears, no death, no crying.**

Revelation—**End-times, Tribulation, Armageddon, New Jerusalem, Satan bound, 1000 years of peace, Satan loosed for a short time, banned forever, the Great White Throne Judgment, New Heaven and New Earth,**

1 Thessalonians 4:13-18; 1 Corinthians 15:52—**Rapture**

1 Corinthians 2:9—**Eye has not seen-Ear has not heard-for those who love him.**

1 John; Romans 10: 9-13; Acts 2:37-39; 2 Chronicles 7:14—**Salvation**

Isaiah 59:1—**His ear not heavy that he can't hear-Arm not short that he can't save**

John 1:1-14—**The word became flesh**

Romans 3:10-12—**None good—No not one.**

Revelation 21:8—**Hell**

John 14:2—**I go to prepare a place for you ... many mansions**

Isaiah 25:8-9—**Heaven and salvation**

Luke 16:19-31—**Rich man and Lazarus—Memories in heaven.**

Ephesians 1:7; Colossians 1:14; Titus 2:14; 1 Peter 1:18-19; Isaiah 44:22—**Redemption**

Genesis 3—**Adam and Eve. Power of choice.**

Jeremiah 1:5—**"Before I formed you in the belly, I knew you ... ." You Matter!**

Jeremiah 29:11—**Purpose**

2 Corinthians 5:17; 1 Peter 2:9; 1 John 3:1-3; Isaiah 43:1; Romans 8:14-15—**Identity**

Isaiah 65:25—**New Jerusalem-Animals**

Revelation 21-22—**New Heaven and New Earth**

Genesis 1:27—**Created in God's image**

Isaiah 49:16—**Carved in the palm of God's hand**

Ephesians 4:32; Matthew 6:14; Colossians 3:13; Psalm 86:5; Mark 11:25; Psalm 32:1; Matthew 6:15; 1 John 1:9; Hebrews 8:12; Isaiah 43:25; Ephesians 1:7-8; Colossians 1:13-14—**Forgiveness**

Acts 3:19; Matthew 9:13; James 4:8; Luke 15:7; Acts 17:30; Mark 1:15; Acts 2:38; Luke 13:3; 2 Chronicles 7:14—**Repentance**

Luke 22:31-32—**Satan desires to sift you—Jesus has prayed for us ...**

John 10:10—**Satan comes to steal, kill, destroy—Jesus gives us life abundantly**

1 Peter 2:24—**By his stripes we are healed**

Revelation 1:18—**Jesus has the keys of hell and death**

Romans 6:9—**Death has no dominion over Christ**

Matthew 16:18—**Gates of Hell shall not prevail against it**

Joshua 24:15— **Choose you this day**

Romans 3:23—**All have sinned and come short of the glory of God ...**

Ephesians 2:4-9—**By grace you are saved by faith ... not of our works lest we boast..**

Matthew 19:14—**Suffer the little children to come unto me**

Ephesians 6:12—**We wrestle not against flesh and blood but against spiritual wickedness**

1 Kings 8:27—**The heaven of heavens cannot contain you**

James 4:1—**Your life is a vapor that appears for a little while and then vanishes**

Matthew 11:28—**Come to me, all who are heavy laden, and I will give you rest.**

Psalm 91:1—**He who dwells in the secret place of the most high ...**

Philippians 4:7—**The peace of God which passes all understanding ...**

Revelation 4:6; 15:2—**Sea of Glass ...**

Revelation 21:1—**New Heaven and New Earth—here there is no more sea**

Revelation 22:1-2; Ezekiel 47; Zachariah 14:8—**River of life, tree of life, fruit**

Psalm 34:7—**angel of the Lord encamps round about them that fear him, and delivers them**

Psalm 91:11—**For he shall give his angels charge over you to keep you in all your ways.**

2 Chronicles 6:18—**Heaven cannot contain thee ...**

Isaiah 5:14-16—**Hell has enlarged itself.**

Isaiah 11:6—**The wolf also shall dwell with the lamb ... .**

Matthew 6:24—**You cannot serve God and mammon.**

Romans 10:3—**Establishing your own righteousness.**

Psalm 139:14—**I am fearfully and wonderfully made**

Ephesians 1:14—**Earnest of our inheritance**

John 11:23—**Thy brother shall rise again**

Mark 13:32—**No one knows the hour, not even the angels**

2 Timothy 3:5—**Having a form of godliness, but denying the power thereof**

Matthew 25:41—**Hell for devil and his angels**

Songs Mentioned in Book:

"We'll Understand It Better By and By" by C. A. Tindley (1905)

"Redeemed" by Fanny Crosby (1882)

"At Calvary" by William R. Newell (1895)

"Amazing Grace" by John Newton (1779)

"Our Lord's Return to Earth Again" by James M. Kirk (1894)

"I'll Fly Away" by Albert E. Brumley (1932)

"I'll See You in the Rapture" by Charles Feltner (1974)

"The Old Country Church" by J.W. Vaughan (1934)

"Beyond the Sunset" Written by Blanche and Virgil Brock, Lyrics written by Albert Rowsell (1935)

"It Is No Secret" by Stuart Hamblen 1950

Remember Me........

~by Marsha Barth

Look past my broken body
Look past what eyes can see
Look deep into my heart
At who I used to be.

Look past your tears of sorrow
Look past the veil of pain
Look deep into my heart
And the love we'll share again.

Look past this life that passes
Look past this mortal clay
Look deep into my heart
Where my love for you will stay.

Look past the sting of death
Look past its finality
Look deep into my heart
Where my soul is now set free.

Look past the years you'll miss me
Look past that great divide
Look deep into my heart
For there's joy on heaven's side.

Look deep into my heart
I'm not so far away
Look deep inside your heart
For you will find me there today.

https://www.youtube.com/watch?v=c9iGixej1R8